A DIVIDED DUTY

A DIVIDED DUTY

A Novel

CAROL WHITE

Library of Congress Cataloging-in-Publication Data

White, Carol
A Divided Duty

p. cm.
Paperback ISBN: 978-0-9975470-4-7
Ebook ISBN: 978-0-9975470-5-4
Library of Congress Control Number: 2017932484

10 9 8 7 6 5 4 3 2 1
First Edition, March 2017

 CITRINE PUBLISHING

Boca Raton, Florida, U.S.A.
561.299.1150
Publisher@CitrinePublishing.com
www.CitrinePublishing.com

Also by Carol White

Hidden Choices

From One Place to Another

Sitting Pretty

Coffee Breaks

For LNR

TABLE OF CONTENTS

PART ONE

PART TWO

PART ONE

"O beware, my lord, of jealousy; It is the green-eyed monster which doth mock the meat it feeds on."

Chapter One

TAKEOVER

"My noble father, I do perceive here a divided duty."

Otto Blackmoor, Jr., squirmed in his seat while trying to decipher the handwritten notes penned by his late father. Otto Blackmoor, Sr., may have been a brilliant businessman, but going through piles of unorganized scraps of paper left his elder son befuddled. Otto hardly felt ready to take over the company, but the loyalty he owed his late father's legacy outweighed his own business capabilities.

I'll have to make it work. Everyone is depending on me now. Especially Ivan.

Otto glanced at his watch for the third time in the last ten minutes, and decided to plow through more scribbles before resorting to the scotch his father kept in the wet bar of the wood-paneled office. He stood up to stretch when his younger brother, Ivan, gave his customary three-tap knock on the open door.

"Got time for me, Otto?"

"Of course," he said, happy for the distraction. Ivan, although a notable slacker when it came to work, had the ability to brighten everyone's day, even a week after their father's death.

"Beautiful skyline and you sure can't beat this fall weather, especially after a long hot summer. Yeah, the city of brotherly love; perfect for us, wouldn't you agree?" Ivan said, gazing out from the floor-to-ceiling windows. "I'll take Philly over Manhattan any day. No wonder Pop liked having his office on this side of the building. And speaking of offices, this one certainly suits you; but tell me, isn't his seat still a little warm?"

"Ivan, I'm exhausted, so don't start. It's been a rough week and you must realize that we had to get back to work. Father would have wanted it this way."

"Are you kidding? Do you really believe that? 'Father' would have wanted a national holiday proclaimed for him, not everyone back to the grind so soon. And when did you start to call him Father? Otto, let me give you a little piece of advice: loosen the hell up and take that stick out of your ass."

"Nicely put. I'm trying to manage the best I can," he said, with a telling sigh. "Pop was all about the company, and his image. He probably would have wanted to be immortalized on a postage stamp, but all our employees were here the day after the funeral and it's important to show support for them."

"I'll give you that, but don't stress yourself out," Ivan said, casually pacing back and forth on the threadbare carpet. "Speaking of which, why on earth did your beloved Casey Michaels call a two-hour meeting this morning? Just to hear you tell him he was the new Vice President? Come on, your head must have been spinning."

Otto walked over to the bar, not caring what time it was, and poured two drinks. He knew Casey's promotion would be a source of frustration and disappointment for Ivan, but his reasons for doing so were obvious to anyone who worked at Blackmoor Industries.

"Do we have to go into this now?" Otto said, handing his brother a cut glass tumbler filled with ice and scotch.

"I know what you're thinking; Casey knows his stuff. All I'm saying is that it could have waited, plus you didn't have to make the meeting all about him and how much extra work he was willing to take on. How do you think that makes me feel?"

"I guess I should have mentioned that I want you to stay on as Assistant Manager," Otto said, checking his watch again to make sure it was at least past four-thirty.

Ivan took his late father's seat behind the desk, which was piled with papers, and placed his drink on a tattered notebook.

"How the hell did Pop sit here? An electric chair has to be more comfortable," he said, rising and holding up his glass for an informal toast. "Like the song says, it's five o'clock somewhere. I hope Pop's not looking down at us for breaking his cocktail hour rule."

"Relax. And don't worry about a job. You'll always have one here while I'm in charge."

The brothers clinked glasses, and each took a healthy swig of the premium brand their father treated himself to, one of his few extravagances.

"I should hope so, with Pop leaving the business entirely to you."

"I had no control over that. I found out the same way you did—at the reading of the will. I'd assumed he'd split the estate and business fifty-fifty," Otto said, feeling guilty and hoping to heal Ivan's bruised ego.

"I can't believe Pop made his lawyer the executor of the will, and not one of his sons."

"Oh please, I already explained that to you, and Rodrigo was probably better equipped to handle it. He took care of all Pop's affairs and was only carrying out his wishes. Like I said, how was I to know what Pop planned? He never discussed anything of importance with me."

"I find that a bit hard to believe seeing that you were the Vice President of the company, and now

President. Otto, can I be frank? I was hoping for a promotion to your old job as V.P., or even Casey's job as General Manager. How can you have an Assistant Manager without a General Manager? Jesus, this is the most confusing shit!"

Otto chuckled at his brother's fractured business sense, which would actually have been logical had Ivan not been such a screw-up.

"You have a point, but I'm not ready to make all those decisions quite yet. I thought I covered that in this morning's meeting. Moving Casey up was out of necessity. There's a lot of business coming in, and I don't want to lose continuity. Let me work on your situation," Otto said, praying he'd be able to figure out something palatable to his younger brother.

"I get it, but I hope you don't mind if I remind you about it in a couple of weeks. In the meanwhile, a raise would sure help...the promotion can wait. Emily's great with budgeting, but even she's getting frustrated. There's only so far to stretch a buck. Things are going up, not down."

"You don't have to lecture me about that. My wife tells me the same thing. Desiree and I have plenty of expenses too. Ivan, listen to me for a minute and try to understand. I just took over the business and I need a little breathing room," Otto said, trying to modulate his annoyed tone.

"Whatever you say, oh, big brother of mine," Ivan said, not wanting to miss an opportunity to bait Otto.

"You can skip the sarcasm," Otto said, wishing he'd have ushered Ivan out of the office five minutes after he entered, before their conversation degenerated into an argument.

"And you can watch that temper of yours. I was only stating my case. There's gotta be some extra money in the business to give your little brother a boost in pay. I'm sure Casey got a raise," Ivan said, sounding like a spoiled brat.

Otto sighed the sigh of a put-upon big brother before answering.

"Frankly, I haven't gotten that far, and he hasn't asked."

"Yeah," Ivan said, with a derisive snort. "Casey's always the consummate gentleman."

"Dammit, Ivan!" Otto said, slamming a book down on the desk. "Why the hell do you have to bother me with this crap now? And yes, Casey will get a raise because he's crucial to this company. We're dead without him now that Pop's gone."

"Otto, take it easy. I didn't mean anything by it. I guess I was a little sarcastic. Sorry," Ivan said, pulling back.

"Oh geez, Ivan, I'm sorry too. All this pressure about being the head of the company. I depend on Casey a lot. The truth is that I never asked Pop to make me Vice President. It's no secret that Casey was a lot more qualified. He's the one who should be running this operation, but 'Blackmoor & Sons' was always Pop's dream, even though he never bothered changing the name," Otto said, mollified.

"Hey, I didn't ask to run the joint, just to be bumped up to the next level. Anyway, haven't you ever heard that blood is thicker than water?" Ivan said, continuing to goad his brother.

"I hear about it all the time. Buddy, let me ask you a simple question. Why does every discussion we have end in a ridiculous row over nothing? Especially today when my nerves are shot to begin with?"

"Buddy? I haven't heard that since I was a little kid and you used to cart me around on your bike. Made me feel special. So, let me apologize for the second time in two minutes. You're right. I don't want to argue, plus you're still bigger than me," he said, smiling as he went into a boxer's stance. "Watcha got on me? Ten, fifteen pounds? You could deck me any time."

"I've also got fifteen years on you, and who said anything about fighting?" Otto said, hoping to extend an olive branch. "Let's focus on the business at hand. There are some changes that need to be made around here. Pop never wanted to modernize. We've been working in the dark ages. We're lucky we have computers and people who know how to work the damn things. You're pretty good in that department."

"Remember when I tried to show him how we could keep an inventory online? You'd a thought I was describing a space shuttle. We could've made things so much smoother around here. Wish he'd listened to me on that," Ivan said, his eyes downcast remembering how his father had given a "puh" before dismissing his son, and the idea.

"That was wrong of Pop. No harm in trying something new. I should have stuck up for you, but he didn't listen to me either. Maybe now we can finally enter the computer age, better late than never. You know, of course, that I'm as bad as he was and you'd think my wife would be tech savvy at her age, but she's clueless too. It's great that you're such an expert," Otto said, meaning it. He'd been impressed with his brother's skills, watching him work on his laptop that he brought to the office since their father refused to pay for another computer.

Chapter Two

REAL ESTATE

"I pray you, turn the key and keep our counsel."

Otto, Sr., had indeed run the company with little room for updating or improvement. It was a miracle that Blackmoor Industries made a decent profit, but hardly what it was capable of earning had it been modernized. His catch phrase was that the steel business should be run with an iron hand. Because his prices were so competitive, the customers didn't protest the handwritten invoices, or the fact that there were only two old computers to receive orders. All follow-up was done by telephone. On the positive side, Otto, Sr., employed more people than was truly necessary, and salaries were higher compared to the rest of the industry's. Along with a generous vacation schedule, the staff received upgraded health and holiday benefits. Nobody complained, or if they did, it was after hours at one of the local pubs. Otto, Sr., may have been cheap in his personal life, but was quite the opposite when it came to business.

With Ivan being so much younger than Otto, computers came naturally to him. Because Ivan was a late-in-life baby, their mother spoiled him with every new cyber invention or game that appeared on the market, and Ivan's innate ability to figure them out, even as a child, was remarkable. In comparison, and maybe by choice so as not to be competitive with his younger brother in at least one area, Otto used an old desktop model for limited functions. Buying a smartphone was out of the question. He was all thumbs, in the wrong way, when it came to using one the way Ivan did without even looking at the keyboard. He and his wife, Desiree, called each other ten times a day, but Otto had to admit that the calls sometimes came at inconvenient times and his wife wasn't all that understanding when he was short with her.

Computers were definitely Ivan's area of expertise. If he'd had a freer rein while his father was alive, the company could have substantially increased business and profits.

"How about if I write up a few proposals," Ivan

said, hoping to stay in Otto's good graces. "But I can hold off if it's too soon. We've waited this long—another month won't matter."

"We should be making the best of our situation, so there's no reason why you can't begin to scope it out, and I promise to consider that promotion for you, and a raise. Desiree tells me all the time that I need to take a bigger salary to cover our growing expenses with the house."

"I can only imagine. That's quite a ticket you have," Ivan said, tempting his brother into a conversation about a subject he knew Otto would rather forget.

"Why the hell did I ever let her talk me into buying that damn white elephant?" Otto said, falling into the trap.

"Wasn't Pop against that move?" Ivan continued, knowing full well that their father warned Otto about taking on the innumerable repairs an old house would certainly warrant.

"That's all I heard about for months from him. I suppose that's why I bought it. To spite him. I wish he'd have been more supportive and then maybe I would've listened to him about the house, but my wife loved it, and I guess I had to prove that I was capable of making my own decisions outside the office. He sure as hell didn't let me make any here."

"The place does have charm," Ivan said, unable to hold back a laugh, encouraging the camaraderie between them.

"Yeah, right," Otto said, joining him in the joke, "but I'd rather have walls without holes and windows that open than whatever charm lies beneath those damn creaky floors."

The house in the exclusive Bryn Mawr suburb may have once been beautiful, but years and probably decades of neglect had turned it into a monstrosity, however strong the bones were. Otto's wife, a former Realtor before their marriage, saw the potential of the rambling home in one of the best areas of the Philadelphia suburbs and insisted that with some TLC, they could spin it into a masterpiece. More important, the house had four bedrooms to accommodate the two children they hoped to have, plus a maid's room for the nanny Desiree would insist upon, and whatever else her heart desired.

"Aw, it'll be beautiful when it's all fixed up. Desiree has a good eye for that," Ivan said, falsely singing his sister-in-law's praises. "Emily and I have been trying to scrape enough together for a down payment on a house because our condo is beginning to feel a little tight. I'm not complaining because I was grateful Pop saw fit to buy it for us, although he never let me forget about it. At least it's giving Emily and me a chance to build up our savings."

Otto was fully aware that their father was almost forced to buy the condo for his younger son after the couple was evicted from their apartment for being in default of three months' rent. By the time Ivan told his father about the lapse, it was too late to reinstate the lease and Otto, Sr., bought the small condo for the couple and arranged to auto-pay the monthly maintenance.

The brothers never discussed the situation because Ivan felt embarrassed by his failure to support himself and his wife, and Otto didn't want to add to the emotional load. He also knew that the condo was in Emily's name because, although it was fully paid for, their father still didn't trust that Ivan wouldn't sell it in exchange for a handful of magic beans. Emily had a good business head, and after the leasing debacle, which he didn't tell his wife about until the eleventh hour, she convinced Ivan to let her manage all their financial affairs.

Emily had been employed by Blackmoor Industries as their human resources director, but her husband's antics humiliated her once too often and she left to accept a position at an art gallery. She had majored in fine arts in college, and not only was she thrilled about her new situation, but she also turned into a top-notch salesperson. Her income helped pay off their credit card and other debts, and she convinced Ivan to offer to take over the maintenance payments from his father. Otto, Sr., although impressed by their wanting to take on more responsibilities, continued to pay the monthly fees.

Otto, Sr., had little respect for anyone's abilities, except Casey and his daughter-in-law's. Emily and her father-in-law got along famously and he mentored her in money matters until she had a full understanding about creating and sticking to a budget.

Emily was a beautiful woman who adored her ne'er-do-well husband, even with his shortcomings. Maybe she'd looked beyond the present into the future when Otto Sr., would no longer be around, and she and Ivan would be the recipients of half the large estate, including the business. Ivan was a good-looking man with a physique he worked on almost daily, and the two made a stunning couple. Emily had large green eyes and lustrous auburn hair that fell to her shoulders in loose waves. Her slim waist was accentuated by perky round breasts, and legs that never stopped. At five feet and nine inches in height, she was only slightly shorter than Ivan. Some men might have felt insecure walking next to a tall woman who wore four or five inch heels, but he relished looking at his sexy wife knowing what brewed beneath that fiery exterior. Her sexuality was tangible and Ivan knew it was only for him.

Emily was as shocked as much as the others upon learning that everything had been left to Otto, and by marriage his wife, Desiree. When Emily first met Desiree, after she'd been introduced to Otto, she considered her a perfect match for her brother-in-law and encouraged Otto to take the relationship seriously. Working quickly, Desiree bedazzled him, and with Otto smitten, Emily was pushed to the side.

It wasn't so much Desiree's looks that made her attractive, but rather her stately posture and expensive trappings. Desiree was of average height with thinning brown hair made fuller by extensions, highlighted by the best colorist Philadelphia had to offer. With lessons from a well-known makeup artist, she learned to apply cosmetics with a natural touch, yet still able to bring out the golden glints in her hazel eyes. She shopped in all the designer departments with a personal stylist so even when going for a walk she was totally put together. While Emily dressed to show off her body, even a little too revealing at times, Desiree had dressed for the job she wanted: the wife of an important man with at least as much money as she had.

There wasn't a man with a breath left in his body who didn't desire Emily physically, but it was Desiree they wanted by their side for the long run. She exuded style and good breeding, everything that a successful man, or one on his way up, needed.

Whatever Desiree wanted, she received, including a four-carat emerald-cut diamond engagement ring, while Emily's had been crafted out of a tiny stone taken from a pin left by her late mother-in-law. At the time she didn't care because she and Ivan were very much in love.

The two couples socialized when Desiree and Otto began to date, but it was rare that the four got together after the marriage.

Now with Otto Sr., gone, Desiree's status was elevated from rich to extremely wealthy and she was no longer interested in hanging out with her in-laws.

Chapter Three

THE WORLD IS YOUR OYSTER

"Hail to thee, lady! And the grace of heaven…"

It had been months since Desiree had browsed through the gallery where Emily worked. Knowing it was her day off, she spent over fifteen thousand dollars on two paintings, giving Emily's co-worker, Brent, the commission. Emily politely confronted Desiree who simply said it was an impulse buy, and that she couldn't arrange her schedule according to Emily's. Brent had been almost embarrassed by the situation and offered to split the commission with Emily, but she refused knowing that her young associate needed the money as much as she did.

Desiree's agenda consisted of having her hair and nails attended to weekly, along with Pilates and Zumba classes, shopping, and going to charity luncheons with women who fell into her upgraded station in life. There was no fit for Emily save for an occasional outing. Desiree admitted, if only to herself, that she was jealous of her sister-in-law's beauty, and the chemistry between her and Ivan. Even though Desiree loved Otto, and their sex life was satisfactory, although not frequent, there was no denying the sparks that flew between Emily and Ivan whenever they were together.

Desiree had a difficult time erasing the image of the two the time she'd unwittingly come upon them in the corner of the supply room when she'd gone in search of linen towels for the executive restroom. It was after five and Bianca, Otto's secretary, had left for the day, so while waiting for her husband to finish up in his office she decided to grab a few fresh towels and lay them out herself. The door was ajar but right before Desiree entered, she heard muffled cries—almost moans—so she hesitated before going further.

Peeking in, nervous that a stray cat or worse had found its way in, she caught a glimpse of Ivan leaning back against a bookcase, eyes closed and grunting with obvious sexual satisfaction. Desiree's eyes moved downward to the source of his pleasure and saw Emily on her knees with Ivan's penis inserted deep in her throat. Instead of moving away, Desiree inched forward for a full view and remained glued to her hiding place. She witnessed Ivan shoving his engorged member in and out of his wife's mouth while pushing her head in rhythmic motion. A final thrust brought him to climax and it was all too apparent that Emily delighted in the episode. Desiree backed away a few feet trying to compose herself, and decided the linen towels could wait until Bianca refilled the basket in the morning.

Although Desiree had enough street smarts to know that most men reveled in fellatio, Otto never seemed particularly interested in it and had actually pulled her up to him the first time she decided to try it. She had been coveting a gold and diamond watch, and thought this extra trick would move it along. Otto, being generous to a fault, and also prideful of his wife's indulgences, didn't need the sex act. All she had to do was ask, which she did, and by dinner that evening the twenty-thousand-dollar watch was on her wrist.

Before Desiree and Otto were married, and while she was still hoping for a proposal, they double dated several times with Emily and Ivan. Desiree knew that Ivan wasn't the most productive member of Blackmoor Industries, but socially he was a lot of fun and their dinners out proved to be quite pleasant, that is until the evening that Desiree dubbed "The Oyster Affair." The four had gone to the Oyster House on Sansom Street and decided to sit at the bar where they ordered their favorites, taking time to savor each treat, served raw, slippery and delicious. Desiree noticed Emily feeding one to Ivan and decided she could be playful as well. Otto was amenable to her offering and slurped down a Bluepoint. The two bottles of champagne Otto ordered flowed, and their laughter increased exponentially.

Patrons crowded in at the bar, pushing the two couples closer together to make room for them to squeeze in. Desiree continued to feed her husband and Emily did the same with Ivan. For a moment, Desiree was uplifted knowing that she and Otto would become close with Ivan and his wife, which would please her husband, and that she would no longer look down on or envy her sister-in-law. Otto was making a toast when she noticed what Emily was doing. Emily had worn a mini skirt that evening with stiletto sandals without tights underneath even though there was an autumn chill in the air. Emily, while looking Ivan in the eye, was reaching under her skirt and bringing back up two fingers of her wetness which she placed on his waiting tongue. Licking his lips, Desiree heard him say, "Got any more of that?" Anyone standing nearby would have assumed he meant the oysters. Only Desiree realized what had happened.

She never told Otto what she'd witnessed, but any further invitations from Emily and Ivan were turned down with a litany of excuses, except for the rare lunch or coffee get-together, which Desiree accepted to keep peace at home.

Desiree had been a successful Realtor, but she told Otto she'd never be able to keep that up while attending to remodeling their new home. He bought her pitch hook, line and sinker, and even though the broken-down resale gave him nightmares, he had to admit that his wife had taken control of finding a reliable general contractor so perhaps the place would begin to shape up after all. Otto now earned more than enough of a salary for them to live the way Desiree wanted so there was no need for his wife to work if she chose not to. Blackmoor Industries was one of Philadelphia's leading corporations and Otto wanted his wife to be well prepared at all times for the many events where their presence was requested, and not off with some client trying to sell office space.

They'd recently decided to try for a family and Desiree had told him that stress was the worst thing for women in their thirties who were trying to get pregnant. He swallowed that too.

Chapter Four

BUSINESS

"She is indeed perfection."

The brothers continued to chat amiably and discussed business plans they felt needed to be pursued. Otto was still nervous about increased expenses in the company, but felt he owed more of an explanation to Ivan.

"Money's tight for everyone, but I promise to think about that raise. I was just going over the salaries when you came in," Otto said, taking a deep breath before continuing in a sympathetic tone. "Buddy, I never realized that Pop paid you so little. Even our secretaries make more than that, and Bianca probably has a Swiss bank account on what she takes home."

"Yeah, but at least I had a job. It didn't make me feel terrific, but what choice did I have? I actually told him, more than once, that we'd both be happier if I worked elsewhere, but that wasn't part of his '& Sons' plan. Luckily, Emily's doing well enough over at the gallery, and believe it or not, I'm secure enough to accept that my wife's salary is bigger than mine and we've learned to live within our means."

"You two have a strong marriage; not every man could handle that. You could have left if you were that unhappy despite Pop's dream of having his sons take over one day. I never understood why you stayed given the way he treated you, not that he treated me much better, but I couldn't very well bite the hand that was feeding me so generously," Otto said, remembering how Desiree had admonished him about ever leaving.

"I never told you this, but I showed Pop a resume and asked if he'd write a letter of recommendation for me to show a few headhunters. I'd drafted it up saying that there wasn't enough of a computer department for me here, and my talents would be far better utilized in another industry. He said he'd take it under advisement. I never got the letter of reference, and he said if I went elsewhere he'd make sure I wouldn't be hired any which way he could. Philly's a big city, but Pop's reputation was bigger."

"Jesus, Ivan, I didn't have a clue about that."

"Hey, it's history. And don't worry about a raise. I won't push you. I'm not glad that Pop's gone, but it's like a weight's been lifted off my chest. I think I'm going to like coming to work now, that is, if you think I can be of real service."

"Of course, I want you here. You're the only person in the office, well, I guess besides Casey—and I know he can be a pain in the ass at times—that I can talk to and not feel like I'm being judged or sucked up to. Why don't you work on a roster of what you think needs to be done and we'll discuss it. Just the two of us. Casey doesn't have to be in on everything."

"I'm on it," Ivan said, with a smile that was actually a smirk if you looked close enough. "With enough modernization, we can probably double our sales in a year or two. We lose an incredible amount of time doing things by hand, the way Pop insisted."

"Wow, double? That's ambitious, but I wouldn't mind giving it a shot."

After refilling their drinks, the brothers went on to review new orders and a few computer programs that Ivan thought would be useful. Otto, as usual, was flummoxed by the details, but understood how service to their customers would be substantially improved by the speed and efficiency these techniques provided.

The two were so deep in conversation that they hardly noticed Casey Michaels standing at the threshold of the door, with Desiree at his side.

"Knock, knock. Hi Otto, Ivan. Look who I ran into getting off the elevator," he said. As usual he was dressed and groomed well enough to be photographed for the cover of *GQ*.

Casey Michaels had been hired by Otto, Sr., ten years prior, and although Casey had never called him by his first name, there was a mutual admiration and respect between the two that was never replicated with Otto, Jr., and certainly not with Ivan. Emily had introduced them having known Casey from her college days, and perhaps that was another feather in her cap regarding her relationship with the elder Mr. Blackmoor. There were times that Otto, Sr., told Emily she should have married Casey when she'd had the chance. Although uncomfortable with the inappropriate suggestion, she laughed it off saying she was perfectly happy in her marriage to Ivan.

Casey had heard the same remark from his boss, and breathed a sigh of relief when Emily resigned her position at Blackmoor's to work at the art gallery. He had no problem openly joking and flirting with

Desiree, but kept his distance from Emily, not wanting to give Otto, Sr., any room for speculation. It was a prickly situation all around and hopefully, Ivan never caught wind of his father's true feelings about Emily's choice of a husband. There was enough animosity between them due to Casey's higher position in the company than Ivan's.

Desiree was a different story. Her father-in-law had tolerated her because she came from a prominent Philadelphia family and he'd seen her name in the society section of *The Philadelphia Inquirer* on more than one occasion. They'd met at a fundraiser for the Opera Philadelphia.

During their conversation that evening, he noticed she was not wearing a wedding band so he took the opportunity to ask if she were seeing anyone. She laughed and said she'd give her eye teeth to meet a man who understood the finer things in life, including her beloved opera. He immediately mentioned that he'd like to arrange an introduction to his elder son, not wanting her to think he was a wolf in sheep's clothing trying to score a trophy wife for himself. Desiree, knowing full well who Otto, Sr., was, masked her disappointment that he was not suggesting a liaison between the two of them, which she would have gladly agreed to. The status and wealth he could have provided for a wife more than half his age would have suited her fine, but Otto, Sr., had lost interest in a relationship during the years after his wife died. That night he was after a suitable match for Otto, Jr.

Desiree Brabant, a career woman and well known in the industrial real estate business, was in her late twenties and had never been married. She was almost twenty years younger than Otto, Jr., whose wife, Claire, had divorced him several years prior. As far as Otto, Sr., was concerned, Desiree and his son were eligible singles and a future marriage was a done deal in his mind. Otto, Jr., thrilled with the prospect of a younger wife after Claire left him, for once took his father's advice and proposed after two months of dating. The fact that Desiree was willing to have children was a bonus. The Blackmoor line had to be continued.

Chapter Five

IVAN THE SPY

"I follow him to serve my turn upon him..."

Desiree entered the office practically collapsing with laughter as she held on to Casey's arm.

"Hi, darling," she said, still giggling. "Oh, hello Ivan," she continued, barely acknowledging his presence. There'd been a cold front between the two since oyster night, mainly on her part toward him since he was clueless about her witnessing the erotic episode. Aside from his animal sexuality, which she knew would never occur in her own marriage, she resented even his lowly station in the company feeling it lessened her husband's position. Without Ivan at Blackmoor Industries, her father-in-law would have long ago made Otto a senior partner in the business and handed the vice-presidency to Casey. It wasn't only the money she was concerned about, even though her husband was well up into the high six figures; it was the stature of the title she wanted for him. For her.

After Otto, Sr., died, Emily casually let slip that Ivan barely made enough to pay their bills, but Desiree simply ignored the information. There was no way that Desiree would ask her husband to give Ivan a raise, knowing how he wasted time in the office. In the meanwhile, she felt that the money Ivan made could have been added into Otto's salary. The house renovations were eating up a good portion of their cash.

She knew her father-in-law had been against the purchase of the Bryn Mawr property, and she would have given up on it had her husband not pressured her onward to be one up on his father. What a hot mess it had turned into, and was now costing way more than expected to cover the basics to make it minimally livable.

"Desiree, hi, sweetheart! Hey Casey, what's the joke?" Otto said, walking over to kiss his wife. As always, she was perfectly decked out.

"Oh, the usual silly stuff. This time it was his impersonation of Donald Trump. You must have heard it," Desiree said, hugging her husband.

"No, I guess I missed out on that one," Otto said, his posture stiffening. He knew Casey meant no disrespect, but seeing his wife draped over his arm and convulsing in laughter was not exactly a scene that thrilled him.

"Hi, Desiree. Casey. If you don't mind, I'm going to excuse myself and clean up the boardroom. What do you want me to do with those folders?" Ivan said.

"Thanks, Ivan. You can leave them with Bianca and I'll get them later. See you soon," Casey said, in a warm tone. Casey had no true affection for Ivan, but treated him as an equal, and as an executive, although his position as Assistant Manager was little more than an errand boy. Casey had witnessed the way Otto, Sr., had treated his younger son, and wanted to try to bolster Ivan's confidence. After all, they were co-workers, and the new boss's brother. With his inflated salary and promotion, Casey couldn't afford to make enemies with anyone in the company.

Before backing out of the office, Ivan turned to Desiree and smiled. "It's so nice to see you again. I hope we can all get together soon. I'll have Emily call you."

"Yes, let's try to do that," Desiree said, icicles dripping from her voice.

Otto felt the atmosphere in his office sharply change after his wife's nonchalant reply to Ivan and decided to take the chill out of the air.

"Ivan, stop by my office before you leave tonight; there's a few more things I wanted to ask you about. Computer stuff. You're the expert and I wouldn't mind a lesson or two," Otto said jovially, trying to smooth over his wife's indifference.

"Sure thing. See you all later," Ivan said. He scooted out of the room, but lurked nearby behind a column to hear any follow-up conversation that might pertain to him.

Desiree picked up on her husband's placating tone and realized she'd been overly bitter with Ivan. She immediately softened and called after him.

"Ivan," she said. "Is Emily meeting you…oops, he's gone."

"Yes, my little brother was born with sneakers on his feet. So, sweetheart, what's the occasion that brings you here, not that I mind."

"Honey, you said I might be able to redecorate your new office so I stopped by to take another look. And to try to convince you to say yes."

Casey, Desiree's biggest fan, chimed in.

"Redecorating? Not a bad idea. You might want to get one of those ergonomic chairs and ditch this old metal thing that probably kills your back," he said.

"I don't know how my father could stand it. So, tell me more."

"I didn't want to say much for the moment because it's just in the planning stages, at least in my mind, but I'd love my husband to give me the green light," she said, looking around the room. "Nothing's been changed here in years."

Despite the stress and aggravation of the past week, Otto let out a good old-fashioned belly laugh.

"I can always count on my wife to lift my spirits.

That's entirely true. Pop was living in another era; I think we all agree on that. I guess you can go ahead. Please make sure you find a reliable designer and I'll look over the estimates.

Always anxious to do the right thing, Casey added his thoughts.

"I think I know the right person for that. Listen, Otto, you can nix this if you want, but we might get a much better deal if we redo all four of the executive offices."

"You mean a quantity discount? Makes sense since we'll probably have to do it sooner or later. Why don't you get all the figures while you're at it and we'll see. I don't want to go overboard. Now how about letting me get some work done so we can afford all this new fancy stuff."

"Of course, darling. I'll go grab some coffee and wait for you," she said, going over to her husband and kissing him on the cheek. "I'll hang out in the lounge till you're ready to leave, or we could stay and eat in town? How's that?"

"Ha! Any excuse not to cook! But that's not a bad idea. I won't be too much longer. Let me wrap up a couple of things and I'll come get you."

Casey immediately took hold of Desiree's arm, ready to escort her down the hall.

"Come on, I'll walk with you. I'll check back here before I leave but first I'll get some coffee for your gorgeous wife."

"Thanks, Casey," Otto said, bristling at the familiarity in the compliment. "That she is. See you in a bit, sweetheart."

As soon as Ivan heard that Desiree and Casey were leaving Otto's office, he practically jogged away back to his office.

No sense letting them wonder what I'm hanging around for.

Desiree was reluctant to leave although she'd missed her coffee at lunchtime and felt the need for a hit of caffeine. Her instinct was to approach her husband again about redoing the offices before he put it out of his mind. Releasing herself from Casey's grip, she turned back toward Otto.

Chapter Six

TEMPER, TEMPER

"Who can control his fate? 'tis not so now."

"On second thought, you go ahead, Casey. I forgot a few things I need to tell my husband. Have a good evening," she said, placing her handbag on one of the chairs that was sorely in need of reupholstering. Her new leather Prada bag with its signature hardware looked out of place on the old chair, which was exactly the effect she was going for.

"Sure," Casey said, looking somewhat disappointed. "Have a nice evening."

"What did you forget, or did you just want a few minutes alone with me?" Otto said, as soon as Casey was gone.

Desiree sidled up to her husband, her breasts brushing his upper arm.

"Always that," she said, nudging him into the right mood. "But, darling, I did want to know how you honestly feel about redoing the offices. I don't want to spin everyone's wheels if you're going to say no, I mean, if you've already made up your mind to keep things as they are."

Otto disengaged himself from his wife and then slammed a book down on the desk as noisily as he had done with Ivan.

"Dammit! Why are you always second guessing me? You haven't even gotten preliminary figures yet. How am I supposed to know if I'll accept it? And don't I have enough to think about right now with Pop being gone? I swear sometimes I don't know where your head is at."

Realizing she had appealed to Otto at the worst possible moment she quickly replied, "Yes, you're right. I'm sorry I even mentioned it."

She sighed knowing that once Otto fell into his anger mode there was no stopping him.

"We already have one money pit!" he said, affirming her thoughts.

"It's our home, and we bought it at a good price. I said I'm sorry to have brought it up in the office today. Can't you please let it go?"

Otto went on as if he hadn't heard his wife's apology.

"No one else wanted that piece of crap and the

owners must have been thrilled to unload it to a couple of suckers, and my dear, we've put almost fifty fucking thousand dollars into it already and it still looks like it's falling down. If you can tell me why we needed a ramshackled old house with four bedrooms yet..."

"Otto! Stop! We both wanted the house because of the size and location, and with room for a guest house later on. Didn't we agree that once we have a family, if we're lucky, that we'd need the space? I'm sorry, for the third time! This was obviously not the moment to bring up redoing the office. I'm going to get some coffee. If you feel like becoming a human being again, let me know," she said, hoping that a slight guilt trip would help Otto control his wrath toward her.

To make matters worse, the house, which she realized too late, had been a terrible investment. Desiree's expertise had been in commercial real estate, not residential, and she knew, after the fact, that buying the house had been a major mistake in judgment. Her new secretive plan was to do a minor fix-up and flip it, but how could she share that with her husband in the mood he was in? Hopefully, he'd be happy about it once she spoke to a few brokers and got a bit more intel on the project. She would manage all the details, but for the moment, it was one baby step at a time with Otto. She had to pretend that the renovations were coming along well unless she could persuade him to lighten up and listen to how she wanted to manage the house going forward.

"I'll see you later," she said, figuring there was no sense in continuing the discussion without being sure of how to proceed with the house situation. She turned on her heel and walked toward the door.

"Wait, don't go like this. I'm sorry, sweetheart. Please don't upset yourself. It's all this pressure with the business; I can't handle anything else right now. And if you must know, Ivan's asked for a raise. That's what we were discussing before you and Casey came in, and now with possibly redoing the offices, I can't…"

Before she could control herself, she blurted out, "Ivan! That blood-sucking freeloader! Why should he get a raise? I thought you'd fire him now that your father is gone."

Her outburst was all Otto needed to restart his rampage.

"I cannot and will not fire my brother. We had a long talk this morning and Ivan's going to step up. He could probably have run the entire order department if Pop had given him the chance instead of hiring that outside company to do the computer work for us. And you cut him off before when he was simply trying to make a date. You were so rude it was embarrassing. I can't remember the last time the four of us went out together. You seem to forget that he and Emily stood up for us at our wedding."

"Yes, and I did that to please your father."

"Damn it! Stop picking things apart. My god,

sometimes you're impossible. He's my brother. You don't have to like him, but you sure as hell have to be civil to him."

"I don't dislike him, he can be quite charming, and Emily's a doll," Desiree said, speaking in half-truths and biting her tongue to avoid revealing her real distaste for the couple. "I don't want him to take advantage of you like he did with your father."

"Why don't you let me handle my brother and you can concentrate on fixing up the house. I know it'll be perfect even if it is costing a small fortune. Forget what I said before," he said, pulling her close. "I mean if we had to do it over again, I wouldn't have offered to buy it, but now that it's a done deal, we can move forward. More important is to get this baby-making thing down."

"It'll happen, darling. We've only been trying a couple of months," she said, wondering if she should proceed with her new idea about their recent purchase. They were comfortable enough in their townhome, which was also located in the tony upscale suburb of Bryn Mawr although not in the million-dollar-plus estate section.

"Let's keep practicing till we get it right," he said, kissing her deeply.

Sensing an opportunity, Desiree seized the moment to present her thoughts about the house.

"Darling, I need to tell you something," she said, disengaging herself from his arms. "This is humiliating for me since I was in a related business, but no time like the present. I know you're under a lot of strain, so maybe this will lighten the load. I was going to wait, but because of what you just said here goes. I want to get rid of the house. I'm not going to bore you with all the details, but please tell me it's the right thing to do."

Otto laughed and stepped forward to pull his wife into a tight embrace, almost lifting her up.

"Yes, yes—a thousand times yes! Get rid of that old dog any which way you can and I don't give a shit if we lose money on it."

"I can finish up with the contractor for another ten or fifteen thousand to make it presentable, with plenty of curb appeal, and then put it back on the market. It's in a prime area and I bet a young family, or even a builder, will snatch it up. For sure we'll break even and more than likely, make back everything we've put into it, plus a few bucks."

"You're certain about this?" he said. "I don't mean the money part; I won't hold you to that, but just that we can sell it."

"Pretty sure. I have enough contacts in the residential market, and they'd scramble for the listing. Properties in that spot have gone up at least twenty percent since we bought it, and frankly, I'm happy in our townhome. I mean we'll have to buy a house when we have a family, but for right now, can we stay put?"

"This is amazing. From a money pit to a money-maker? Go ahead, and thanks for getting us out of it. That's the best news I've heard all day. Do you have any idea how much I love you?"

"I think I have an idea, and I'd be glad to show you how grateful I am when we're in bed tonight," she said, once again leaning into him with her well-toned arms wrapped around him.

"I'll look forward to that. And I promise, if I hit my target, we won't have to name our son Otto the Third!"

"Thank you for understanding and I'm so sorry I got us into the mess in the first place."

"It was partially my fault also. Should have listened to the old man about the house because he sure as hell was right about fixing me up with you, my beautiful miracle worker," he said. "Go ahead with getting rid of the house and you have my blessing."

"One more thing and then I must get an infusion of coffee. You're absolutely right about the way I've behaved with your brother. I'm going to give Emily a call. She's at the gallery and I'll see if they can meet us tonight as long as we're staying in town. From now on I'm going to make a real effort with your brother."

"That's my girl. How about letting me get back to work?"

Chapter Seven

BROTHERS BOND

"On some odd time of his infirmity, will shake this island."

Ivan, who'd returned to his coveted hallway spot after he noticed that Casey had left by himself, decided to again eavesdrop for another minute before re-entering Otto's office. He casually intruded, his eyes scanning some folders he used as a prop.

"Okay, boardroom's cleared out. Oops, sorry folks, didn't mean to interrupt your moment."

"Not at all. I was just leaving," she said, being cordial. "Ivan, Otto and I are going to stay in town tonight and have a bite to eat. Do you think you and Emily would like to meet us? We haven't been out together for ages."

Having overheard that part of the conversation, he nonetheless acted pleasantly surprised by her familiarity, and rose to the occasion.

"Sure. The gallery's only fifteen minutes away, and she was meeting me here after work anyway. Sounds great. Thanks, Desiree."

"Okay then, see you in a bit. I'll give Emily a call as soon as I get some coffee; I'm positively wilting. Oh, Ivan, would you hand me my purse, please?"

Desiree gave her husband another kiss, and left the two brothers to carry on with the business at hand. She felt relieved that Otto hadn't blown up at her news about re-selling the house. Hopefully, they could recoup the money they'd already spent and if they made a profit, it would go right into the proper home she envisioned. Desiree realized that the old house had been a serious blunder, and a situation she should have stayed away from, but Otto was determined to defy his father.

The house was in a perfect location, and it's not that Desiree didn't want to live in Bryn Mawr, where her family was from, but after visiting her society friends who resided there she decided that building something from the ground up would be a much better idea. Certainly bigger and better than the place she was going to resell. The townhome would do for now, but not if they were blessed with children. The three levels would be inconvenient, and there'd be no room for a nanny and a live-in housekeeper, both of which she planned on, plus a guest house and a pool. She knew they would build a masterpiece whether they were parents or not.

"You know, sorry I was such a prick before. I've been thinking and I kind of enjoyed being at that meeting today. It felt good to be treated like part of the team," Ivan said, sitting in the chair that had recently been occupied by a handbag that probably cost a week's salary for him. Emily had told him about the purchase after Desiree showed it off to her on one of the rare occasions they met for lunch.

"You are part of the team now."

"Thanks. That means a lot to me."

"Meetings can drag on sometimes, but they're important. I've been known to drift off listening to all those reports," Otto said, hoping to sound empathetic.

"The truth is that I was so pissed because Pop never included me in anything of importance, and I ended up taking it out on you. I know I messed up in the past, but trust me, that's all behind me now. I might take a few lessons from you on how to conduct myself," Ivan said, hoping to flatter his brother, "but I never want to be the same uptight stuffed shirt Pop was."

Otto rose from behind the massive oak desk and came around to stand closer to his brother.

"Be careful what you wish for, buddy. I hate to admit it, but I'm pretty sure the staff likes you more than me. Why don't we learn from each other," Otto said, patting his brother on the back.

"It's not that I didn't love him; you know I did, it's just…well, you know…"

"Take it easy on yourself. Pop was tough on both of us. Don't you think he was always looking over my shoulder? Double-checking my work? Questioning me on every decision? Of course, you loved him. So did I, but let's face it, he wasn't the most loving guy in the world. That was Mom's job. You know you were her favorite, the baby."

Ivan chuckled remembering how his mother had coddled him, maybe so much so that he rarely ended up doing things for himself.

"Yeah, the surprise baby, although I'm pretty sure Pop thought of me as a mistake. I think about Mom a lot. She died so young and Pop never got over it. It seems that's when he stopped being a real parent."

"You're right about that. Sometimes I felt more like an employee than a son to him, and not even an employee that he liked. I hope I can fill his shoes. No question that he was the best in the business, even with his archaic ways."

"You're going to do fine. Do you mind if we get back to this morning's meeting for a minute?"

"Sure, fire away."

"How do you think it went, I mean, my input, at least the small amount I was able to squeeze in."

Otto had another good laugh from his brother's polite way of alluding to Casey's steamroller style.

"So you noticed? Yes, Casey does tend to run on and on, but you came up with some pretty good ideas. He's a yakker alright, but we need him. And, Ivan, I was a real prick before too. I didn't mean to blow up, but the adjustment, the responsibilities, the financials; they're enormous. And that damn hulk of a house, but want to hear the latest? You're not going to believe this, but now my wife wants to get rid of it and stay where we are for the time being. That woman is going to drive me crazy, even though I have to agree with her."

"What? But you guys are fixing it up," Ivan said. "I thought you were going to make the move right after Christmas."

"Nope, now she wants to gussy it up cosmetically and put it on the market. Flip it. We agreed that it was an albatross from the beginning. Another thing Pop was right about. Frankly, I breathed a sigh of relief when she told me. The townhome is fine although it won't be long term. I hope we can unload the monster soon, so we can build something else in a different location."

"There's nothing like new construction. You don't have somebody else's headaches. I'm sure Desiree has connections to sell it. But I thought you wanted to stay in Bryn Mawr. It's totally upscale. My wife would kill to move there."

"We'll definitely stay in the area, but it'll have to be in the estate section," Otto said, ignoring his brother's last comment. "Desiree is right about a new house. Once we have kids we'll need more room and a yard."

Ivan almost fell off his chair and hoped his feeling of shock didn't show on his face. Not previously having heard that part of the conversation left him dumbstruck.

"Kids?" he squeaked out before quickly composing himself. "Wow, what great news. I didn't know you were thinking that way. Emily and I've been talking about having kids too. That's why we hope to be house-hunting soon, but probably not over in Bryn Mawr, although wouldn't it be kind of cool if we lived closer to each other once we have children?" Ivan said, pressing his point about location.

Otto could have helped Ivan and Emily finance a small home in the same community, but wasn't sure of how he felt about living near his brother, and ignored the question. Being in the same office for business was one thing, but they traveled in different social circles, and too much closeness might work against the families.

"You've been married for how long now? Ten years, is it? I guess it's time. I'm going to look like the grandfather in the group, but who cares."

"Nah, you don't look anywhere near your age. Emily's been wanting to have a baby forever, but I never felt secure enough to be a father. Frankly, I never knew from one day to the next if Pop was going to throw me out on my keister. I have to be sure that I can take care of a family. Otto, I want to deserve a promotion…not get bumped up because I'm your kid brother."

"Of course. I have a good feeling about our being in the business together. We have a fantastic bunch of employees, loyal and hard working, and it shows in the profits. Pop made all of this happen and you know how important loyalty was to him."

Chapter Eight

IVAN SETS THE SCENE

"To beguile many and be beguiled by one..."

I van took in a deep breath before continuing the conversation. It was a toss-up as to how his brother would take the news, but hoping to prove his allegiance, he decided to chance it. He'd have to handle his remarks with kid gloves.

"I agree about what you said regarding loyalty," Ivan said, falsely grimacing as if he were in pain. "There's something I've thought about confiding in you, but only if you promise not to go postal on me, and I'm not sure this is even the right time. So much has gone down already this week, but since you and I want to be on the same page, I figured it's best to give you a heads up on the situation."

"Confide? Sounds serious. Go ahead. What is it? You and Emily are okay, aren't you?" Otto asked. Although Ivan had always been Peck's Bad Boy, Otto was still concerned about his welfare. "What's on your mind?"

"It's Desiree."

"Desiree? What the hell? Oh, wait a minute. I think I know what you're getting at and I'll be straight with you. I know my wife hasn't always been…uh, warm to you. I'm glad you mentioned it, because we not just a minute ago talked about how we seem to be estranged…socially that is…from you guys. She admitted that she's been neglectful with making plans, mainly because the house has taken up so much of her time," Otto said, quickly inventing a reasonable excuse. To put it plainly, he knew that his wife had been a total bitch when it came to interacting with the couple.

"I told her how much faith I have in you, and how things are going to be different around here. Get this; it was her idea for us to have dinner together, so let's try to have a new beginning all around. I think you're going to see a big change in my wife's attitude."

"Listen, I understand all that and figured you're probably the one who had to talk her into dinner because I know that Desiree has had her problems with me. You have to realize how thrilled Emily and I were when you married her. We knew it was a match the first time we met her, but that's not what I'm talking about."

Otto sat back down and either ignored or didn't absorb what Ivan was trying to tell him.

"I never thought I'd meet anyone after Claire left me until Pop made the introduction. I've always been grateful for that and I think it pleased him. I realize how perfect Desiree is for me even though she talked me into buying that shit box of a house. Claire and I were never right for each other, but she was a good wife. I wouldn't have broken up the marriage, but I sure as hell gave her cause to walk."

"Please listen to me for a minute. It's more than Desiree's attitude and believe me, the way I've acted in the past, I sure as hell couldn't blame her. So, like I was saying…" Ivan tried to continue but Otto broke in, going on with his sentimental reverie.

"I can't imagine my life without her. Once you and I both have kids it'll be even better. Holidays together, barbeques; we'll be a real family again. Philly's not that big a town," Otto said, not wanting to encourage any thoughts of their being neighbors. "Here's another thing I've been thinking about. After Rodrigo gets Pop's estate all straightened out, I'll split everything down the middle, the way it should have been. It might take a while because the will has to finish going through probate, but I'm on it. Can't believe Pop set it up that way instead of putting it all in a trust we could get at."

Now Ivan was in a fix. He knew once his older brother set his mind to something, like taking care of their finances, he'd make it happen. In this case, it would be monumental for him to receive half of his father's huge estate, and if Otto believed the information he was about to hear, perhaps that would speed things along, but what if it worked against him? He dared not let Desiree's obvious dislike of him interfere with getting his rightful share.

Why did I even mention the bullshit with Desiree? He's not going to forget that I started the conversation and when he finishes telling me how great his wife is I'm going to be forced to continue unless I can pull a rabbit out of a hat to throw him off base. I need that money from the estate! I better play the grateful little brother and suck up to him big time.

"Otto, oh my God, how can I thank you for that? I felt pretty down that Pop didn't leave anything to me. To put it bluntly, I felt like I'd been kicked to the curb and stomped on. I guess I must have been a hell of a disappointment to him," he said, with a hangdog look trying to appeal to his brother's benevolent side. Sure, he had felt cheated, but it hadn't come as a surprise to him. The old man never treated the two sons equally while he was alive. Ivan hadn't expected that to change after his death.

Otto rose and again put an arm around his brother's sagging shoulders.

"I don't think that's true. I think he probably forgot to change his will, and he knew I'd always take care of you," Otto said, softening the truth.

"Yeah, you've always been pretty damn good at that. At least now I'll deserve it."

"That was wrong of Pop, but we'll fix it. So let's move on. What's the problem? Something about Desiree or did we straighten out that situation? Look, I know she's much younger than I am, but we're in love. Oh, sure, we have our battles, but I've been given a second chance and I don't want to screw it up. We've been so happy. That's why we're starting to talk about having a family. Desiree tells me a child will keep me young. We'll see how that works out."

"It'll keep," Ivan said, trying to maintain the status quo, and his brother's good will.

"Nah, let's get it out in the open. I'm sure it's nothing that can't be fixed. Go ahead."

I'll take the chance; he wouldn't go back on his word to split the estate, would he?

"You're right, might as well, but please listen to me for a minute and try not to blow your stack," Ivan said, pausing to summon up his courage. "I hate to be the one to tell you this, but I think Desiree may be screwing around on you."

The silence in the office was deafening as Otto backed away from his brother.

"What in the hell are you saying? That's my wife you're talking about. How dare you…" he managed to blurt out, his lips in an angry snarl. He clenched his fists, almost holding himself back from striking his brother.

"Whoa! Don't kill the messenger. If you'd calm down I can tell you what looks suspicious to me, but if you'd rather not hear what I have to say, then forget it," Ivan said. Had Otto not been so riled up he might have noticed that his younger brother's voice was almost melodramatic.

"Of course I want to know now that you've started this crap. Go ahead. Tell me what it is you think you know."

"That's just it. I don't know anything for sure. It's what I saw. Casey was coming on to Desiree before, and she wasn't exactly pushing him away. I was turning down the hall so they didn't notice me," Ivan said, before taking a brief pause. "Otto, it's not the first time I've seen them like that."

"My God! Are you kidding me? That's the most ridiculous thing I've ever heard. Those two always joke around. Everyone knows that. They do it right in front of me, and yes, sometimes they take it a bit too far, but you heard them laughing right here in my office before and it's always over some absurd thing. My wife's a great audience," Otto said, trying to compose himself.

"Listen, you can believe me or not, but Casey's a young guy, good-looking and a sharp dresser. It didn't seem appropriate, for lack of a better word, to me."

"I know exactly how old Casey is," Otto said, enraged with fury. "Ivan, if this is an attempt to have me get rid of him, it's a damn bad idea."

"I'm not totally blind to the hierarchy here. I already figured that you'd move Casey up and truth be told, he's the best man for the job, blood or not. Like you said, he could probably run this place single-handedly. I guess I got a little bent out of shape when you moved him up instead of me, but there's no way I'm ready to handle that position. Frankly, I'm happy staying put."

Although Otto seemed surprised to hear his brother's admission about the promotions, he was secretly pleased that Ivan didn't want to bite off more than he could chew. Maybe his little brother had more grit than he'd been given credit for. Otto calmed himself before continuing the conversation.

"That was my plan; moving you both up, but I didn't want to do it all at once. I thought taking one step at a time was the right way to handle it. We discussed all that and I thought you understood."

"I get it. You're under enough pressure; you don't need more from me."

"But this business about Desiree, it's just not possible."

Ivan had to bite his lip to suppress a grin when he realized that Otto was actually mulling over the possibility instead of dismissing it. Now was exactly the time to apply a little reverse psychology.

"Forget about it. Like you said, they were probably just horsing around. I'm sure there's nothing to it," Ivan said, playing the good guy. "I'm sorry I even brought it up. What a jerk I am. Geez, I'm lucky I have a job here at all."

"You're my brother. You'll always have a job here," Otto said rather grandly. "We're going to work together to build this business."

"That's what I want too."

"I swore when I asked Desiree to marry me that I was going to leave all my jealous bullshit behind, along with Claire's divorce papers. That's what really broke us up—my wanting to know her every move, who she was with, where she was going. I had a fit if she even linked arms with a friend at a dinner party or a charity event. I was a jealous fool and for nothing. We might not have made it as a couple, but we stayed faithful to each other over the course of our marriage."

"Otto, listen to me. I always liked Claire, and I know you had your crazy moments, which drove her away, but let me tell you something. You sure as shit don't want to start that with Desiree. She won't put up with it for one second. Really, Otto, I never should have said anything. I guess I feel a little protective of you because of all the strain you've been under. You've got nothing to be jealous about with Desiree. She loves you, but I will tell you one damn thing and there's no question about it; Casey's a major flirt. She was probably being nice to him because that's how she was raised," Ivan said, thinking about how condescending she'd always been to him and Emily.

Otto was almost trance-like as he sat back at his desk and stared at his wife's picture in the silver frame she'd surprised him with for his fiftieth birthday.

Chapter Nine

THE PLOT
THICKENS

"He holds me well; the better shall my purpose work on him."

"I knew it was too late after Claire left, but I tried to get her back anyway; promised that I'd change, but she didn't buy it. Who needs to start over at this age, but that's history and I'm not going to be that same jerk with Desiree. We already had words before we smoothed it all over. I can't seem to control myself."

"You've made some mistakes, you're human, but at least you learned from them. Again, forgive me for bringing it up. It's forgotten as of now. Done. Let's get back on track. Business!" Ivan said, letting the thought of his wife's dalliance with Casey linger on.

"Don't be sorry. I'm sure you were torn, but it was your duty to tell me. I guess I'd do the same for you."

Seeing his chance at further manipulating his older brother, Ivan chimed in with another one of his obsequious statements. He'd memorized an entire list of compliments to flatter his brother with and knew exactly when to pull one out.

"I always forget how perceptive you are. That's exactly it."

"And I do appreciate it," Otto said, buying into the sweet talk. "Sorry I blew my fuse at first. I've really got to get a handle on my disposition. Can't go around exploding over every little thing, but now that you've opened the can of worms, you better tell me what else you know."

"I don't think I should say any more," Ivan said, with a beleaguered sigh. "How's your blood pressure been lately?"

"Ivan, please. My pressure is fine. Just get it out in the open."

"Okay, like I said, I don't know anything for sure, but it looked like it might be something more than just fooling around."

"But Desiree's never given me any cause whatsoever to be jealous."

Ivan began to play his brother with his well-crafted push me/pull you game.

"Maybe I'm reading more into it because of the way Casey looks at Desiree. I'm sure it's nothing. I told you to forget it. I was ready to let it drop but you insisted on details."

"If she ever left me, for any reason, I don't think I could go on."

"Don't talk like that. Desiree loves you. It's my overactive imagination. Let it go. Hey, whose leg do I have to hump around here to get a drink? Let's break into the old man's stash of primo scotch," Ivan said.

"In a minute. Hear me out first. I'd like you to do something for me. Keep your eyes and ears open but don't let Desiree or Casey have a hint that you're keeping tabs on them. If there's anything at all to this, I need to know. Like you said, it's probably just a harmless flirtation, but I'd feel a whole lot better if I knew for certain that it wasn't more than that."

"Smart plan. I can arrange to do a little simple detective work and report back to you, but for now, how about that drink? I think we've earned it."

"It's a bit early," Otto said, as he picked up Desiree's photograph again before walking over to the built-in bar and pressing the touch latch. The door sprang open revealing a bottle of scotch, a pitcher of water and an ice bucket, both of which Bianca kept filled, along with several old-fashion glasses.

"Like the song says, it's five o'clock somewhere," Ivan said. "Come on. One little drink won't hurt."

Otto couldn't hold back a smile because Ivan started to sing the song he'd just alluded to, and was dancing around the office trying to cheer up his older brother.

"Oh, Ivan, what would I do without you? You're the bright spot in this miserable week we've just been through. Uh oh, Pop's supply of booze is getting low; I'll have to pick up another bottle. Bianca does enough for me; don't want to make her into an errand girl. You know, Pop always had a drink at the end of the day. Hold it, buddy, don't try for any sympathy because you weren't asked to join him. My invitation must have gotten lost in the mail too," Otto said, and laughed despite the dark cloud that lingered overhead.

"Good one, Otto. I was about to call you on that. I feel good about our future, let's start our own traditions and celebrate. Forget what I told you before, but like you said, I'll keep an eye on things so we can be a hundred percent sure. Then, let's kick ass around here and grind this company into high gear. Once we've crossed the bridge into the twenty-first century we'll increase our profit margin at least fifty percent. I guarantee it. "

"I'll take your word on that. Thanks, Ivan. I didn't realize how much your support means to me, but I do now and since we're drinking, we might as well throw something good into the mix. I'm officially making you General Manager, and I'll put in a nice raise for you. I asked Bianca for the payroll this morning because that was something else Pop refused to share with me. Like I told you, I never realized how little you were being paid."

"I managed," he said, shrugging his shoulders.

"You can't pay for a brother's loyalty," Otto said, his voice beginning to crack. "And, there's really no reason to wait what with your new duties in taking over the computer department—we're paying a fortune outsourcing more than half our work."

"Thanks. Pop never listened to me about that and I know for a fact that I can coordinate the department at least as well as it's being done now. I can't wait to tell Emily. My wife's a major worry wart when it comes to money, so she's going to be jumping for joy."

"Emily's a good woman. She and Pop had a special relationship. Remember when she worked here? Let me tell you something…the two of them had a drink together at the end of the day at least twice a week. Once I started to walk in thinking he'd ask me to join them, but instead he motioned for me to close the door on the way out. Can you imagine?"

"Emily was his protégée of sorts, learning all his business tricks," Ivan said. "He was broken up when she quit, which honestly was mostly my fault, because he wanted to train her to be one of the higher ups. She told me he was the best mentor she could have asked for."

"Emily is certainly bright, that's for sure. How's she doing at the gallery?"

"You can ask her yourself because she's on her way

here. I told her we'd go out for a burger, so she'll be happy that you're joining us," Ivan said, adding a little more scotch to his glass. "I'm glad you set it up, I mean, having us all go out tonight."

"Desiree said she was going to call Emily to fill her in. Let me ask you something. I've noticed a distinct chill in the air when the two of them are together. Any input there?"

"Probably because Desiree's not my biggest admirer and Emily's gotten the brunt of it, but I promise, that's all going to change. You won't regret giving me a chance, and for now, put that nonsense out of your head about Casey. Maybe we can fix him up with that hot secretary of yours. Let's drink to the business, and to us, two members of the Lucky Sperm Club."

Chapter Ten

COCKTAIL TIME

"The execution of his wit, hands, heart..."

"**B**oy, oh boy, that scotch really hit me. Mind if I shut my eyes for a few minutes?" Ivan said, taking a seat on the small sofa in Otto's office.

"Not a bad idea. I think I'll join you. Honestly, that's exactly what I've been doing all week. I tell Bianca it's a power nap," Otto said, and sat down near his brother.

With the combination of liquor, their father's death and coming back to work, the two fell asleep almost instantly.

It was about ten minutes later that Otto opened his eyes, and gently shook Ivan's shoulder nudging him awake.

The brothers chatted amiably about Ivan's new area of expertise, and although Otto didn't understand even the basics of the programs Ivan suggested, he had enough confidence in his brother's ability to oversee the department.

Because of the fifteen-year difference in their ages, they'd never hung out together as kids except on those occasions when Otto carted his little brother around to the playground or a local baseball game. Otto was happy they were now becoming real friends. He'd speak to Desiree about her interaction with her sister-in-law because with the two families hoping to become parents, there'd be no room for animosity.

The brothers were so engrossed in conversation, and still a little tipsy from the alcohol, that they didn't notice Casey standing at the threshold of the office until he tapped on the door.

Casey Michaels had dark chestnut hair and piercing blue eyes. With his finely sculpted face and perfect physique, he could have been a stand-in for the *Magic Mike* movies. Casey was a topic of casual gossip among the women at Blackmoor Industries, and there were always a few, including Bianca, who openly flirted with him eager to be asked out on a date. Casey kept his distance. He was hoping that his current secretive relationship would become more serious, so except for friendly chatter, he disregarded any hints or come-ons from the female employees.

Casey had mentioned to Otto that he didn't date anyone from within the company because he didn't consider it professional behavior. There was no reason to explain further.

"Just wanted to say good night again. I didn't mean to break up anything," Casey said, holding on to his Burberry raincoat and Mark Cross attaché case.

"Not at all. Ivan and I went a little overboard with cocktails, so we took a nap—like two kids. Casey, why don't you let me pour you a drink because I want you to hear the news before I make a formal announcement tomorrow. I've decided to make Ivan our new General Manager. It's what my father would have wanted: for his two sons to work side by side," Otto said, going to the bar. "You can throw your stuff on the sofa unless you're in a hurry."

Casey was supposed to connect with his love interest to set up a date, but he couldn't very well turn down the boss's offer to celebrate with them. He'd step up as he always did, and as was expected.

"Thank you. And I second the motion. Congratulations," he said, trying to put some enthusiasm into his celebratory remark. "Actually, Ivan, why don't you stop by my office so I can catch you up on a few open projects. Guys, I hope I can speak frankly. I was very flattered when you made me Vice President, but if you feel your brother is the man for the job, please don't think you'd offend me. I support any decisions you make," he said, knowing full well that Ivan wasn't capable of taking over the vice presidency. Office boy would have been a more appropriate title.

"Thanks for the vote of confidence, but Otto here knows what he's doing. Just beware, Casey, 'cause I'll be your shadow for the next few weeks finding out everything about your former job," Ivan said, with an underlying tone of sarcasm, which Casey ignored.

"You can't scare me," Casey said, a bit too strongly. "I'll welcome it. No problem. I'm glad we're all in this together. You know how much I admired and respected your father. Everyone here did."

"Yes, he was a wonderful man. Honest and loyal to his employees, and to his family," Otto said, hoping his words didn't reveal any hidden agenda.

"Otto, are you alright? You look tired," Casey said, with concern. "You better get some real sleep tonight and not just a nap."

Ivan decided to speak up for his brother to keep the conversation as normal as possible. He couldn't let Casey have even an inkling of what Otto had asked him to do.

"Oh, it's all this pressure about my big brother taking over the company. He's totally stressed. That's why I suggested a pre-dinner cocktail. How's yours, need a refresher?" Ivan said, hoping Casey would guzzle what was left of his drink and take off. There were a few more seeds of deception Ivan wanted to plant before the end of the day.

"Ivan's right," he said, and took few sips of the drink

mainly to be polite. He never much cared for the taste of scotch. He was a vodka martini man. "You're going to be a wonderful leader. Everyone's rooting for you. Okay guys, if you don't mind, I'm going to head out."

Casey picked up his briefcase and with his raincoat over one arm, said goodnight to the brothers and was almost free of the conversation when he bumped into Emily who'd just arrived. He was already fifteen minutes late for the prearranged call, but couldn't be impolite to Ivan's wife, who was actually a good friend of his.

Unfortunately, Emily was overly sensitive about how people treated her, mainly due to Desiree's disrespect, and he didn't want to hurt her feelings by dashing out. They'd had more than one conversation about the boss's wife, and he'd tried to convince her that she must be misconstruing Desiree's behavior toward her. Although Desiree was undoubtedly attractive, she was no match in beauty for Emily; perhaps it was a simple case of jealousy.

"It looks like I got here just in time. Cocktails? Hi Casey. Hi honey, Otto. What are the three of you up to?" she said.

"The boys are celebrating. I'll let your hubby tell you all about it," he said, trying to inch his way out.

"Casey! Hang around. She'll wait for you," Ivan said, slightly drunk now and trying to embarrass the new Vice President. He obviously couldn't continue dropping hints to Otto about his wife now that Emily had joined them, so he decided to make the bachelor late for whatever he was trying to leave for. "Hiya, babe, come on in and have a drink with us. I know you've had Pop's scotch before."

"We don't want to keep Casey; it's been a long day," Otto said, hoping to cover up for Ivan's brash remarks. "But finish your drink first. Emily, how are you? What's new in the art world?"

"Isn't anyone going to tell me what's going on around here?" she said.

"Sure, honey, but first, how was your day? Any sales?" Ivan asked.

"Today was decent, but in general, it's slowed down this year. There are weeks that the gallery doesn't get more than a couple of lookers. Hardly anyone's buying art, I mean the big pieces, in this economy. I'm still doing fine and I love being there, but working on commission in today's market isn't the greatest. Believe it or not, the small prints and greeting cards are our bread and butter these days. Brent pushes those for house gifts, birthdays and such, but I know it's tough for him."

"We sure miss you around here; maybe these two can talk you into coming back to work with us," Casey said, sipping the last of his drink and preparing for a getaway.

"Emily knows she can always have her job back. She was the best office manager, or whatever they're calling it these days, that we ever had. It's not as glamorous as working in an art gallery, but it's a steady salary. How about it?" Otto said.

Ivan refilled his glass and fixed a drink for his wife. He was staggering, and almost tripped on the small area rug in front of the bar.

"Just think, honey, if you came back to work we could always meet in the coffee room for a quickie."

"Ivan!" she said, taking both drinks from her husband and putting them back on the bar. "I think you've had enough. And why are you drinking? What's it all about?"

"Sorry, babe. I didn't realize how powerful this stuff was. Not sure how the old man handled it. Otto, got any snacks around here?"

Casey saw his chance and broke in. "You better get some food, speaking of which, I'm pretty hungry myself. I'll stop on the way home and pick up my usual take-out; you know, a bachelor's dinner. Good night all. Desiree's still in the coffee room. I'll tell her Emily's here on my way out."

Casey grabbed his coat and briefcase, and sped out the door.

"So, tell me. What's the celebration about?" Emily said.

"Otto and I were toasting our new relationship," Ivan said, regaining his composure.

"Emily, I think you should meet our new General Manager. Your husband."

If Emily was surprised at the turn of events she covered it up nicely before congratulating her husband.

"What great news. That's awesome. I didn't think you'd make that change so soon, but it really is fantastic. Congratulations, honey and thanks, Otto. I know Ivan won't let you down."

"Of course, I won't let him down," Ivan said, annoyed that his wife had added a note of incredulity to her response.

What the hell is that about?

"Why would you even say that?" he said, trying to keep the aggravation out of his voice before recovering. "Oh, I get it. Sorry I was a little rambunctious before. That's not going to happen again. And more good news; Desiree and Otto are joining us tonight for dinner. Did she reach you?"

"Yes, she called, and right when I was in the middle of trying to close a big sale, which was my only one this month. I've got to teach her how to text. The two of you are impossible with technology," she said, in jest, but with an underlying tone of impatience.

"I promise to teach them; one lesson and it'll be done," Ivan said, speaking up before his wife let her true feelings come out. "So, how about it, dinner?"

"Sure, please come with us. We were just going over to Monks," she said.

"Not any more, milady. Tonight we're going to the Ritz-Carlton for cocktails and dinner. How about it, Otto? The four of us haven't gone out together in a while and we've had a tough week. Let's do it up right."

"There he goes again. Money burns a hole in my hubby's pocket. It's a good thing I'm crazy about the guy."

"I think for tonight, he's right. The occasion calls for the Ritz and it happens to be my wife's favorite. I'm pretty sure Pop would have approved," Otto said, his voice filled with nostalgia. "Let me go tell Desiree. Would you mind calling for a table; it's early, we shouldn't have a problem with a reservation. I'll be right back."

Before he left, Otto once again put his hand on his brother's shoulder.

"I have to check something in the mailroom before I pick up Desiree so it'll be more like ten minutes. Make yourselves comfortable," Otto said, a bit choked up and left the young couple in his office.

Chapter Eleven

IS IT HOT
IN HERE?

"O, behold, the riches of the ship is come on shore!"

“The Ritz? I love it there, but it’ll cost a fortune unless your rich brother picks up the check,” Emily said.

“Not necessary although I won’t fight him for it. I’m getting a raise.”

“Thank God! A promotion and a raise. I thought Otto was going to keep a status quo for a while, at least that’s what Desiree let slip the last time she deigned to have coffee with me.”

“Maybe you two can try to work out your differences. The Ritz is right up her alley, so fake it if you don’t feel it, but you might as well enjoy it. We need the both of them. I'm leaving it to you to romance her because Otto and I are like this," he said, crossing his two fingers as a sign of their closeness.

Emily was about to speak, maybe complain about the playacting, but her thoughts changed direction. She wouldn't mind hobnobbing with her sister-in-law and the uppity crowd she ran with. Of course, she could never invite any of them to their small condo, even with the solid art collection she'd amassed over the years. She'd made important connections through working at the gallery and had purchased paintings at deep discounts from sellers who appreciated her taste, and respected her budget. Her father-in-law had encouraged her to form a collection as a sure investment, and even helped her out from time to time with large cash presents for her birthday and on other holidays. She once found a huge bundle of hundred dollar bills hidden in an Easter basket among the colorful foil-wrapped chocolate eggs. The others in the family just got the candy.

"I can do that. I have no problem with Otto, and your dad and I got along so well. I miss him. I know you do also even though he treated you…well, like Desiree treats me. A second class citizen. She's such a damn know-it-all."

"Listen to me for a minute. Desiree doesn't know everything, and she sure as shit doesn't have a clue that I think she's screwing around with Casey. If I can prove it, then Casey's out on his ass, which leaves me second in command, even a full partner, and finally able to get somewhere in this company and make some real money. With Pop gone, Otto's going to start to depend on me more and more, and I'm gonna cut that cord tied to Casey."

"Hold on there, Mr. Big Shot. That doesn't sound the least bit likely. Say what you will about Queen Desiree, but she does love your brother. And he gives her whatever she asks for, including that ridiculous house. I don't think she'd fool around with anyone. She's not stupid. She certainly wouldn't pick someone from the company. What put that idea in your head?"

"First of all, they're going to dump the house and stay in their townhome. Desiree decided to build or look for something more modern in Bryn Mawr, which has the best school district, because they want to have kids. Otto just laid that bomb on me. Why does he need kids at his age? To inflate his ego even more and carry on the Blackmoor line?"

"Slow down. We're going to be part of that dynasty and I'm sure Desiree is pressuring him about a family. She's thirty something and I guess her clock is ticking, just like mine. I think you better back off with Casey because that can't be true. And I wouldn't mind having a place in Bryn Mawr either, so forget the rumors and throw your efforts into business. Once my sales pick up, and with your raise, maybe we could afford a small house there."

"I'm not starting a rumor; I'm only stating what

looks like the facts. I can't close my eyes to the situation. I have a bad feeling about it, and if something is going on, I'll get proof," Ivan said, sounding like a prosecutor. "I don't want anyone taking advantage of my brother."

"Granted, Casey's a great-looking guy, but he wouldn't jeopardize his position here. No way are they having an affair. They're friends, just like he is with me. Maybe you think I'm screwing him too," she said, turning her back on him.

"Oh no, not you, because you know I'm the best in that department," he said, pulling her back to him. "But, my dear, just because you and Casey are old friends doesn't mean you see what goes on here. You're not around when he and Desiree are carrying on in the office."

"What I know is that Desiree is wild about Otto and has been since the day they met, back when she wasn't such a freakin' condescending snob. Please don't go further with this talk," Emily said, pleading with her husband.

"Why do you always take sides against me? Can't you believe in me this once?"

"I love you and I'm thrilled that you've received the promotion and raise, but if you continue on with this crazy story, and Otto gets angry enough, he'll throw you out on your ass. Then where will we be?" Emily went to the bar and picked up the drink Ivan had poured for her earlier.

"Honey, I'm still his kid brother and he always forgives me. That's our drill and has been for as long as I can remember. I screw up and he covers for me. And wait'll you hear this! He's even working on getting me my share of Pop's estate. It won't happen overnight, but at least he realizes what I'm entitled to."

"My god, that would be fantastic, but I'm still asking you to be careful. If we're going to try to have a baby, and look for a house we can afford, you've got to keep this job and stay in your brother's good graces. I'm almost at the point of quitting the gallery. It was great the first few years I was there before the economy went south, but today's sale was the first I've had in a month and I almost lost that one due to Desiree's phone call. It couldn't have come at a worse time, but to keep the peace, I had to take it. It's going to be tough living on your salary until that estate is settled and who knows how long that takes? Maybe I should try to see if there's an opening here in the human resources department, at least until we get pregnant, so we'd be able to save a little more."

"Don't worry about that right now. We'll manage. With my raise I don't think we'll have much to worry about. Stay at the gallery; you love the art world. The economy's picking up and I bet you'll have new customers before you know it."

Emily sipped her drink and put her arms around her husband.

"Oh, Ivan, that's why I love you so much. You always care about my needs."

Ivan embraced his wife, his hands roaming over her slim body. He could almost feel her heat.

"Baby, I know exactly what your needs are because they're the same as mine."

"Ivan, don't start! Not here. Otto will be back in a minute."

Ivan's hands strayed a little further until she forcibly, but reluctantly, pushed him away.

"Honey, I'm begging you; please be careful. Once you get half of your dad's estate, it won't matter who's screwing who, but if you put those ideas in your brother's head now, it can't be good for us."

"Sweetheart, I don't want Otto to be hurt any more than you do. True, she's not my favorite person, but I'd like any woman who'd be good to my brother. I wasn't the one who had the problem with Claire… Otto screwed up that marriage. Desiree and Casey have been in that coffee room when they thought no one else was around. Trust me, you'd have gotten upset too if you could have seen their bullshit. Even Otto asked me to watch them so, he must suspect something."

"How 'bout keeping it on the down-low for now? We're going to need your raise because I don't want to wait for the estate to be resettled before we try for a baby, or a house. If you piss him off, he could hold up the raise, and your share."

"I'm the first to admit that I didn't pull my weight around here, and I know that's why you quit. I embarrassed you, goofing off all the time, but Otto never would've given me that promotion if he didn't trust me, and the raise is a done deal."

"Remember, we depend on your brother's goodwill to keep us afloat, the same way we depended on your father."

"Honey, stop mothering me. Don't you worry. Let me handle this. If there's nothing to tell, believe me, I'll be the happiest guy around. You're right, babe, I'm sure it'll prove to be nothing, but in case something is going on, Otto has the right to know about it."

"Sometimes talking to you is so damn frustrating. Don't waste valuable time chasing windmills," she said, pushing away his roaming hands.

Shit, I've gone too far telling her about my plan. Why doesn't she realize that the sooner Otto fires Casey the sooner he'll give me an even bigger raise, Ivan thought, before reversing the discussion.

"You know what? Maybe you're right. I get these wacky ideas sometimes. I'm going to drop the whole thing. I'll tell Otto I was pissed because I didn't get the promotion at first, and exaggerated the situation. I already said as much to him. I never should have brought it up in the first place. Thanks for keeping me on the straight and narrow," Ivan said, although he had no intention of giving up his plot to get rid of Casey.

"Don't upset your brother. You've got to keep your relationship on an even keel," she said, lecturing him.

"Come on, Emily, don't be angry with me. You did just say you were crazy about me, and look at us, ten years married and we can't keep our hands off each other. Let's go out and have a good time. You look beautiful, and you won't have to check the prices tonight."

"Just use caution," she said, turning her body once again to his. "So, tonight I can have an appetizer and dessert?"

"Sky's the limit and if I can get you tipsy enough we'll see about finishing what we started when we get home," he said, his hands moving to her breasts, feeling her nipples harden.

"Now, when have you ever had to get me tipsy to make love?"

"You know, Otto said ten minutes and that gives us more than enough time for a quickie. I bet you're getting wet for me right now," he said, thrusting his hand under her skirt and pulling down her panties. With two fingers he roughly put them inside her, proving his point and making her moan with lust.

"Just as I suspected," he said, straightening up and licking his fingers. "You're ready for me right now. If you lean over the desk, I'll make you cum in thirty seconds. No one else is around, and Otto's down the hall. I'll hear him coming, but I'd rather hear you."

Without a word he bent her over Otto's desk, unzipped his fly and penetrated her immediately feeling her wetness encompass his hardened member. With one hand on her back to balance himself, he snaked the other around to massage her clitoris, all the while pumping deeply into her. He masterfully brought her to orgasm before having his own climax.

"Jesus, you are one sexy babe," he said, pulling up her panties. She primly smoothed down her skirt while he straightened himself out.

"Ivan, I didn't have my diaphragm in. We took a chance," she said, sitting on the desk, her face still flushed from the passionate coupling.

They pulled their clothing on and Ivan stuffed her torn panties into his pocket. He led her to the office sofa where they sat and waited for Otto to return.

"I bet one of my little fellows is swimming upstream right now. I hope it hits home because at least that'll be one thing we do better and sooner than Otto and Desiree. You are one magnificent broad, and I mean that in the best sense of the word. No way my brother's bending his wife over anything for a hot fuck. They probably do it in bed on Saturday night with the lights off."

PART TWO

*"Why did I marry? This honest creature doubtless
Sees and knows more, much more, than he unfolds."*

Chapter Twelve

BUSINESS AS USUAL

"...my heart's subdued even to the very quality of my lord..."

A few weeks later the office routine returned to normal, and Otto's business and home life were going well. The listing broker for the old house had given them a decent offer from a young couple with school-aged children. The husband was in construction and a handyman's special was a perfect fit. They never could have afforded anything else in the Bryn Mawr area, so both buyer and sellers were satisfied.

Several days after they accepted the offer, and when she knew Otto was in an upbeat mood, Desiree paid him a surprise visit at work. He'd been delighted that she had supervised the minor repairs and painting that gave the property an attractive appearance, and had staged the interior to look warm and inviting. Today, she'd brought up a picnic basket and they decided to have lunch in the executive board room. It was a relaxing hour with delicious food and even a small bottle of rosé wine.

"Darling, let me walk you back to your office; then I'll clean up in here. I know how busy you are and I don't want to take up more of your time," Desiree said. "I'm glad you liked the sandwiches. I decided to try that new gourmet place a couple of blocks from here. It's a little pricey, but…"

"But nothing! I still can't believe we made over twenty thousand on that house so we can certainly afford a fancy office lunch once in a while. The food was perfect, but you're right, I have a mound of papers to get through. I'll see you tonight."

"Sweetheart, don't wear yourself out because I'm ovulating and you know what that means," she said, seductively.

"I know what it meant this morning, but I'm happy to oblige again," he said, and kissed her passionately. "Get out of here before I throw you on the table and do it right now! Who can wait?"

Looks like that profit I made on the house has become a major turn on for my conservative husband, or maybe some of his brother's displays of affection toward Emily have rubbed off.

"We wouldn't want Bianca walking in on us, now would we?" she said. "See you later."

After Otto left she wrote two notes on her personalized stationery. One was for Bianca, who was out to lunch, asking her to clean up the board room and the other was for Casey. She tiptoed into Casey's office, making sure no one was around, and placed the note beneath his calendar leaving part of it sticking out so he'd be sure to see it. Desiree was arranging to meet with Casey in the lobby of the Ritz-Carlton hotel the following week, so the note was only a confirmation. She knew he wouldn't forget their plan. What she didn't count on was Ivan watching her from behind a half-open door.

Chapter Thirteen

RENDEZVOUS

"That he is too familiar with his wife..."

"**D**esiree! Over here," Casey said, trying to keep his voice low. He was standing by one of the elevators at the Ritz-Carlton holding his ever-present Mark Cross briefcase, and a sheaf of papers in his other hand.

"Hello," she said, giving him a peck on the cheek. "My, don't you look very vice presidential."

"Ha! Thanks, and as my first official duty I'm supposed to be meeting a client here, at least, that's what I told Otto. Listen, do you think you could learn how to text? Anyone could have seen that note the way you left it," he said, holding up half of

Desiree's stationery. "I kept this part to remind me to speak to you about it, but tore up the rest and threw it away because the shredder is on the fritz for a change. Luckily, the staff knows that I'm pretty fussy about who goes in and out of my office, something your brother-in-law chooses to ignore."

"I'm so bad at all that tech stuff, but I'm getting a new phone and Emily promised to show me how to do it. She and Ivan keep bugging us to learn so she can teach me," Desiree said, not really caring about what her in-laws wanted. "I guess we should grab something to eat, maybe a sandwich at the bar? Or do you want to wait until after?"

"After. Let's get moving," he said, and pressed the button for the elevator.

Desiree took his arm and whispered, "We're going to have to be super careful that Otto doesn't find out until the timing is right. I don't want to spring anything on him. He's been through enough."

"Once we explain everything to him, it'll work out," he reassured her. "It's best not to say anything yet until we have it all in place. I'm so glad you had time to meet me today, and the Ritz is far enough away from the office so that no one ever comes here for lunch."

"I agree," she said. "We'll take it slow."

"Where's the damn elevator? I don't have that much time and we don't want to be in a rush. I have to be back in the office before my meeting with Otto this afternoon to discuss the new client he thinks I'm pitching."

Neither of them noticed Ivan standing behind a large potted tree taking photos of them with his phone.

Chapter Fourteen

MEETINGS

"…to spend with thee: we must obey the time."

When Ivan returned to Blackmoor Industries after his secret agent job, he made sure that Bianca, who presently served as secretary to both Otto and Casey, was still out to lunch before proceeding with his hunt. Once that had been confirmed, he surreptitiously entered Casey's office and sped through the contents of the waste paper basket, which would be emptied by the cleaning team after six in the evening. He had to get his proof before Casey or Bianca returned.

Sneaking into the fusspot's office is one thing, but pawing through his garbage could get me in real trouble. I've got to find what I came in here for and get out!

Within seconds, he found several pieces of Desiree's stationery. Ivan shoved the evidence, which he hoped would be damning, into his pocket to be read later and refilled the basket with the remaining trash.

Later on, Ivan couldn't help returning to the scene of the crime to look for more pieces of the note. What he'd already read from the first fragments almost spelled out their romance but Ivan needed more ammunition. After Bianca gave him the okay, Ivan entered the office holding on to some folders he knew Casey would be looking for when he met with Otto. They would serve as a handy cover-up should he be caught in the act, which is exactly what happened.

"Hey Ivan, What's up? Were you looking for something?" Casey said, slightly perturbed to find him there. He'd have to speak to Bianca again about letting anyone except Otto or herself into his office.

"Sorry, Casey. Didn't know when you were getting back and wanted to make sure you had these reports for your meeting. Long lunch, huh?"

"Uh, yes, as a matter of fact. Trying to snare a new client took more time than I thought," Casey said, taking a peak at the contents of the folder. "This looks great. I see you've done quite a bit of homework. Thank you."

"No problem. So how'd that client work out?" Ivan said, sticking the knife in another few inches. Unless Desiree was their latest prospective client, Casey was lying through his teeth and Ivan wasn't about to let up on him.

"Not so great, unfortunately, but there'll be others. See you later," Casey said, dismissing Ivan.

"Oh, what a shame. All that time wasted for nothing. Have a good meeting and tell Otto I'll be in to see him before the end of the day."

"Sure thing. I better go over these figures. Please excuse me for now," Casey said, pissed that Ivan was calling him out.

"In that case I'm gonna grab a coffee and help Bianca with a new program before she leaves for the day," Ivan said, enjoying his cat and mouse game. "Better luck next time."

Casey had never entirely trusted Ivan, but he'd come to admire his strengths when it came to computers. Along with Ivan's happy-go-lucky nature, the staff lit up whenever he walked through the office. He'd bring in a cake for anyone who had almost any happy occasion to celebrate, and never overstepped the boundaries of good taste. Quite a change from the flippant do-nothing younger son when Otto, Sr., was alive.

As he looked through the reports that Ivan had prepared for him, he was thrilled that someone else in the office knew how to do this all-important, but deadly dull work. Casey knew another feather in Ivan's cap was his ability to teach others in his department how to hone their skills and learn different programs. Now if he could only teach Desiree and Otto how to text, Casey might even consider inviting him to lunch.

After analyzing the figures from Ivan's report, Casey typed up a review and printed out two copies for his meeting with Otto. He walked down the hall to his boss's office, unaware that Ivan was stealthily following him. He didn't realize that Ivan would be able to listen to every word of their conversation.

"Hey, Otto, is now a good time to go over all this?" Casey said from the doorway.

"Sure, come on in. Before we get started, I wanted to ask how your meeting went with that new client, or prospective client I should say."

"Sorry, boss, but it was a waste of time," Casey said.

"Oh, that's a shame. He's the one you had to meet downtown?"

"Yes. He insisted that he couldn't meet me in our offices, and the meeting took forever, plus traffic was a nightmare. He picked my brain, or what's left of it, and I couldn't cut him off in case he wanted to sign on with us in the future," Casey said, hoping that Otto wouldn't ask for any particulars.

"We can't nail them all. So, do you have those figures for me?" Otto said, glancing at his watch.

Casey breathed a sigh of relief and handed one of the review sheets to Otto and they sat down at the metal work table.

"Your brother dropped by my office with the data and after I condensed it, I ran off copies for us so it's easier to decipher. I believe this is the best deal our supplier can offer, and I think we oughta take it. I studied the estimates with Ivan the other day before he went further, and we both agreed. Take a look and then if you say yes, just sign and I'll get it going."

Otto considered the analysis and concluded that Casey and his brother had done their due diligence, and everything was in order.

"Looks fine to me. Thanks," Otto said. He stood up and hesitated before continuing. "Tell me…how do you think Ivan is doing?"

"He's amazing. Ivan's been like my shadow these last couple of weeks. He's a new man. I'll be frank. I never thought he'd make it this far, but he's the proverbial sponge. He's sure making up for slacking off when your dad was alive. Oh, sorry," Casey said, deciding to stick with the truth and not reinvent the past, but apologized nonetheless.

"Don't be. It's no secret that he was a screw-up. Pop was very hard on him, which didn't help. That's why I wanted to give him a chance. I figured he'd either rise up or totally deconstruct. Looks like giving him more responsibility along with that promotion worked to our advantage."

"Makes my job easier with him so willing to do a lot of the grunt work, and he seems to put everyone in a good mood. He's got that magic touch with people," Casey said, hoping further praise would please his boss.

"That's for sure. He could always make my mother and me laugh, even my father, and you know he didn't laugh at much."

Hearing his brother and Casey applaud his virtues, Ivan decided it was the right time to emerge from the shadows.

Chapter Fifteen

THE BROTHERS CATCH UP

"And give direction: and do but see his vice."

"Hey, Otto. Oh, Casey, didn't know you were still in here. Sorry to disturb you. I'll come back later," Ivan said, knowing full well who was in his brother's office.

"That's okay, something up?" Otto said.

"Nah, just that I'll be working late and Emily's going to meet me."

"I think we're about done for today anyway. I'll get that order in tomorrow, and thanks again, Ivan, for putting it together. Walk out with you?" Casey said.

"If my brother has time I'm going to hang out and catch up with him. I haven't seen the guy all day, except for a quick lunch," Ivan said, placing obvious emphasis on the word quick. "I've been up to my eyeballs installing new programs."

"Fantastic," Casey said, relieved to offer a sincere compliment while ignoring Ivan's obvious dig. "Who knew you were such a geek? You know, Ivan's saving us a ton of money from that company we used to lease out. So, guys, if you don't need me for anything further, I'm going to take off. Have a good evening. Give my best to the girls."

"You go ahead. I think we have a dinner date planned with our wives this evening. Enjoy your weekend," Otto said.

Casey was happy to leave the brothers and get on with his own plans. He'd been thinking about a marriage proposal once all the details had been discussed and ironed out. He'd saved this evening to make up a "pros and cons list" that he would present on their next date. They'd been secretly seeing each other for months; it was time they moved ahead or broke up. There was no telling what would happen at Blackmoor Industries once the news was out. He'd never discussed his personal life with anyone at the office, and aside from Bianca's flirtatious ways, Ivan was the only one who never felt he was imposing by interrogating him about his love life. All Casey ever said was that it was going fine, thank you very much. He'd waited a long time for love and now it was his turn for happiness.

"Sit down, Ivan, let's talk. I can't tell you how happy I am that this has worked out so well for all of us. Casey tells me you're doing a tremendous job and I'm proud of you. And that savings from your handling the programming will go toward redoing the offices, yours included, once that wife of mine gets me the proposals. I don't understand what's taking so long."

"Maybe she's been busy with other things," Ivan said, seizing the opportunity to disparage Casey, but he'd have to wheedle his way in and move slowly.

"I guess you're right. She was going non-stop attending to the house and prepping it for resale. I have to admit she did an excellent job of getting it ready and I think our cost was under ten grand. No wonder that young couple snapped it up. We actually made more than a few bucks on the sale, and thankfully we're rid of it. Leave it to my wife to make a profit out of a white elephant," Otto said, with a self-effacing tone which couldn't hide the braggadocio way he kept his wife on a pedestal.

Ivan felt his blood boil at the mention of another one of Desiree's monetary conquests. While he and Emily struggled to make ends meet, his sister-in-law was flipping houses and not losing a dime. Not wanting to sound harsh, he disguised his bitterness by agreeing with Otto.

"That's super. Glad it all worked out," Ivan said, deciding to hold off on the serious conversation he wanted to have with Otto.

Let him bask in her achievements for a few more minutes until I bring it all down.

"Now if she could only get the office quotes. She's the one who suggested the redo in the first place and then nothing for almost three weeks. I know she'll do a great job so I guess I shouldn't push. We're still celebrating the sale of the house," Otto said, continuing to gloat.

"Otto, the carpeting in the offices is threadbare and this rug is a deathtrap," Ivan said. "We shouldn't put it off too much longer."

Otto pointed to the small woven scatter rug and said, "I remember when Pop brought it in here to cover up the hole in the carpet. Jeez, how cheap can you be? He should have re-carpeted then. For all the money he shelled out on scotch, and his Shakespeare collection, and those stupid bow ties, you'd a thought he'd want something decent in the place where he spent eight hours a day. You're right; I'll make sure Desiree gets on it like today."

"Good idea, and I'll call maintenance and have them get rid of this piece of crap," Ivan said, overly serious before breaking out into laughter. "Pop sure was a cheapskate."

"Didn't mean to go off on a rant there," Otto said, joining in on the joke at his late father's expense. "Come on, have a seat. What did you want to see me about? Business, or do you have good news about someone being pregnant?"

"I'm not here to talk about the business, and we're still working on the baby situation. This is more serious," he said, clearing his throat.

"Then that calls for a drink."

Otto walked over to the liquor cabinet. Cocktail hour had become a pleasant routine at the end of most of their business days. It was a relaxing time for each of them to renew their relationship as brothers. The men and their wives had also become closer as couples now that Desiree had thawed out. The families would survive in business as well as in their personal world. Perhaps that was what their father had arranged; let Otto take over and bring Ivan up to snuff.

"Yeah, I could use one," Ivan said, his nerves jangling with reason.

"Sure thing. We definitely need our liquid refreshment. Let me first say that both Casey and I are pleased with your performance. Casey told me you've been on his tail twenty-four seven learning the job," Otto said, pouring their customary drinks. "Pop's scotch is getting low; this is about the last of it. Do you think Emily could pick up a bottle or two for me? I'd ask Desiree, but she's so busy looking for a new house, and hopefully getting details for the damn office. Emily won't mind, will she? There's a liquor store on the same block as the gallery. She knows the brand."

"Sure," he said, covering up his aggravation at once again being treated like the put upon ne'er-do-well brother. At least it removed any ounce of guilt he might have felt taking a swing at Desiree and Casey. Emily would be pissed as hell, but in the end, she'd do whatever it took to play up to Otto and pad their bank account.

"You wanted to tell me something," Otto said, sipping his drink.

You better slug that drink down, big brother, because you're going to need it.

"Yes, and maybe it'll explain the delay in getting the figures for the office. It's true that I've been following Casey around, but not only for work. You did ask me to keep my eyes open, remember?" Ivan said, licking his chops.

Chapter Sixteen

IVAN STIRS
THE POT

"Thus do I ever make my fool my purse..."

"What? Oh, that nonsense? That was ages ago. There's so much else going on here, I haven't even thought about that conversation. I think I'd know if my wife were cheating on me. We're closer than ever now that we're trying to start a family. I wish it would happen already because I'm exhausted from all the love-making, although I guess I shouldn't complain. Desiree has a bunch of pregnancy tests stacked up, and as luck would have it, we're both far more relaxed now that we've unloaded the house. Apparently, that project was making her overly nervous. It's not every wife who can own up to her mistakes when it comes to money and then cash in on it! Ivan, let's leave her friendship with Casey at that. I can deal with them flirting with each other. It doesn't mean anything. Desiree is totally committed to me and to our marriage."

Ivan added a touch of water and more ice to his drink, wanting to stay clearheaded for the rest of the conversation. He knew his brother might lose his temper, and he wanted to be alert to handle that possibility.

"Otto, listen. Take a look at this. I found it in Casey's office. I only had a few seconds to grab what I could," Ivan said, holding out the Scotch-taped scraps of the torn note.

"Looks like Desiree's handwriting, but I need my glasses to read it," he said, pulling out a pair of Ben Franklin's from the top drawer of his desk. "Let me see. 'Casey, please meet me downtown, and we'll make plans. Same time, same place. I can't wait to see…' Ivan, where's the rest of this? How did you find it and why on earth is it taped together?"

"Dunno…maybe he tore it up and then needed to reread it. But let me explain. When I was in Casey's office dropping off the reports, I happened to notice it. I recognized Desiree's handwriting and wondered what it was doing on his desk. From what I read, I thought you'd want to see it, and I'm afraid that's not the whole story," he said, quickly coming up with a lie about where he'd found the note, and why it was taped together.

Otto wouldn't think much of me going through the trash, and what difference does it make where I found the evidence?

Otto felt a gripping sensation in the pit of his stomach. The note didn't spell out anything concrete, so why was he beginning to worry?

"Ivan, I don't understand, and you probably should have left this where it was. Desiree writes notes to everyone," he said with a strained voice because his antennae were definitely up. Something wasn't right. "They were making plans to meet somewhere? To do what? And what do you mean that this isn't the entire story? What else is there without the rest of the note? I can't simply show it to Desiree and ask her about it. We trust each other. This is bullshit."

"I wouldn't have thought twice about it either, but I saw them downtown together. I'd be happy to give them the benefit of the doubt, even after that, but then I thought I owed it to you to hear me out," Ivan said, proud as a peacock.

"Maybe you better start from the beginning. Put this all in sequence for me because I'm losing track, not that I believe there was any wrongdoing, but I would like to have the facts."

"You asked me to keep an eye out for any funny business so I followed them. They met at the Ritz-Carlton, in the lobby, and while they were waiting for the elevator I saw them kissing and laughing. It didn't look innocent to me," Ivan said, hammering a nail into the coffin of deceit.

"This is crazy and I can't believe it. We've never been happier; at least I thought we were. There must be some mistake."

"I wish I had better news. I'm so sorry. I have a couple of photos, but not sure you want to see them," Ivan said, further manipulating his brother.

"Pictures? Of course I need to see them," Otto said, his breath coming in short gasps.

Ivan held up his smart phone and showed his tech-challenged brother how to swipe across so he could see his wife and her would-be lover.

Otto fiddled with the phone until he got the hang of it. Shock and disappointment showed in his face, and he slumped back into his chair.

"He has his arm around her! And she's kissing his cheek. What's going on?" he said, his bile rising. "What were they doing in a hotel? And at the Ritz yet! That's where we celebrated your promotion. It was to be a new beginning for all of us."

"Yeah, I thought that was kind of low," Ivan said, in a nonchalant way. There was no need to add fuel to the fire. Otto would get there all by himself.

"And to screw around with Casey yet! He pretends to be a loyal employee; he knows how much I depend on him, just like Pop did," Otto said, regaining his composure as he propelled himself up from the chair.

Wildly pacing the room he continued his tirade. "He won't have a job in the mailroom when I'm done with him."

Ivan had to feign sympathy no matter how false the sentiment. He sauntered over to the liquor cabinet to refresh their drinks.

"You better calm down, it was probably nothing," he said. "After all, I couldn't hear what they were saying and maybe it was only a friendly kiss."

"You didn't have to hear anything, dammit! Just the fact that they were in a hotel together says it all, and those pictures. I bet they were going up to a room if they were at the elevator. And kissing? Come on, you know where that leads," Otto said, gulping down the scotch.

"Hey, you better slow down with that drink. You're getting all flushed. Take it easy, and you know, it could have been a friendly peck on the cheek," Ivan said, nervous that Otto's blood pressure might rise to a dangerous level. "I don't think these pictures show the real story because it was mainly Casey who was coming on to her. Desiree was kind of backing off."

Holy shit! This story is going to backfire if I don't calm him down.

"Bullshit! Don't sugarcoat this for me," Otto said as if reading his brother's thoughts. "I'll divorce that bitch. At least Claire never cheated on me. Maybe I should have tried harder to keep that marriage going instead of being screwed over by a younger woman."

Chapter Seventeen

A QUICK TURNAROUND

"What may you be? Are you of good or evil?"

Ivan was in a fix now because his main concern was getting rid of Casey. He had assumed that Otto would become jealous and have it out with his wife, eventually realizing that she hadn't been anything more than a friend to Casey, but firing him would be a good preemptive move. Now Otto was talking about divorce! He had to revise his original plan midstream in order to nip it in the bud. No matter how unpleasant Desiree had been to him in the past, Ivan was in no mood to struggle through a third wife. Ivan and Emily were developing a friendly, if not loving, relationship with Desiree, and she would soon come to realize his importance to Otto as a brother, and accept him as an officer of the company.

Why didn't I think this through? Now I've got to exonerate that bitch of a wife while building my argument against Casey.

"Calm down. You love Desiree. She's going to give you children—isn't that what you've always wanted? Forget Claire. Yes, she was lovely, but she remarried a few years ago, you know that. And let me put this in perspective for you. I've had a little bit longer to digest the situation and here's what I think. I'm sure none of this is Desiree's fault. It's that fucking Casey. Simply tell your wife that you're a little jealous of her relationship with him and you'd like her to back off. Don't accuse her of cheating because we don't have substantial proof. And on the odd chance that it's more than a flirtation you can work that out with counseling, but I don't think it'll get that far," Ivan said, presenting a new and more innocent scenario about his sister-in-law.

"You think it was all his doing?" Otto asked, his voice hopeful for a confirmation.

"Looked that way. I shouldn't have taken those pictures because they're misleading. I hate to say it because I know how much you depend on him, but you're probably going to have to fire his ass."

"I sure as hell hope you're right; that it was all nothing. Could it be that they just ran into each other at the Ritz? Casey was going to meet a prospective client downtown and perhaps Desiree had a lunch date there. She doesn't usually fill me in on all her social outings, so that was probably it. Surely I can ask her about it without getting riled up."

"But what about Casey," Ivan reminded his brother. He was losing ground in his balancing act to have Casey fired.

"Oh, you mean get rid of him? From what you're telling me I don't think I can do that on half a note and a few pictures. Who'd do his job? I bet the whole meeting at the hotel was one big coincidence," Otto said, adding a scoop of ice to his drink and filling the remainder of the glass with water noting that the liquor bottle was almost empty.

"Maybe you better lay off the stuff," Ivan said.

"Yeah, yeah, looks like I'll have to because there's only a few drops left. I need Emily to pick up a bottle—do me a favor and send her one of your texts to remind her. Well, might as well tell me what else is going on because I think I'm really going to need that nap today."

That son of a bitch treats his secretary better than my wife! Let him send his precious Bianca on his errands, Ivan thought, even knowing full well that for the time being he'd have to follow Otto's orders about the errand. *Time to lay it on but good!*

"I've been putting off saying this, but listen to me and then make up your own mind. That guy's been handing over half his work for me to do, in addition to all my other jobs, and he does it when you're not around. I do all the digging and leg work, and then he takes the credit. He's smart, I'll give him that, but he talks a better game than he plays. I could practically take over his position right now from what I've learned. My advice, brother to brother, is to get him out of the company and your life. The way I've seen him act around Desiree; trust me, if he hasn't gotten your wife to bed yet, and I don't think he has, it's only a matter of time. You wanted honesty and I'm giving it to you. It's up to you to make the final decision."

Otto was in a quandary now. What was really taking place between Casey and Desiree? It was unimaginable that they'd carry on practically right under his nose, but he was certainly aware that such things can happen, particularly when it involved a much younger and desirable woman.

"I appreciate everything you're telling me, and I had to know what you saw. Frankly, I should have shut this whole thing down and told you to forget about checking up on them, but I know you had my interests at heart. If there is something brewing, it's better that I find out now before it goes further. I'll speak with Desiree. I'm sure she'll understand my feelings."

The brothers sat in silence, digesting all that had transpired. Ivan had to make Otto realize that getting rid of Casey would be a smart move all around, and he had to drive home his point while Otto was still visibly distressed wondering if his wife had been disloyal.

Desiree couldn't have picked a worse moment to arrive. If she'd have waited even ten minutes more, Otto might have come to the conclusion that he'd set forth in his conversation with Ivan; that it was a chance meeting at the Ritz and nothing more.

Chapter Eighteen

DESIREE DEAREST

"Give me to know how this foul rout began,
who set it on..."

"Hi, sweetheart. There you are, Ivan. Emily's waiting in your office. Can you guys meet us back here in about twenty minutes? I need some private time with my hubby, and then maybe another night out together? I'm dying for one of Monks' hamburgers, with the works."

"Hi, Desiree, sure. See you folks soon."

Knowing how Otto could fly off the handle, and particularly after the heavy drinking, Ivan decided to stay at the doorway, keeping himself well hidden. He'd become an expert sleuth of late.

"What a day I've had. I know we said six, but I came earlier because I need to talk to you. It can't wait. I wanted Casey to hang around to join in the conversation, but he said he had plans." Desiree set down another new designer handbag on an empty chair, but held on to the matching tote bag.

Just as Ivan was calculating how many thousands those two fashionable pieces must have cost, he heard his brother go off the deep end.

At the mention of Casey's name, Otto blew a fuse. He had been prepared to discuss her involvement with Casey in a civil way until it was straightened out. He'd almost convinced himself that it had all been a misunderstanding, and that a simple explanation was in order. Maybe it was the scotch, or perhaps the photos in Ivan's cell phone, or even his Dr. Jekyll's dark side emerging, but there was no question that he was hopping mad.

"I'll bet it can't wait," he said, slamming his drink down so hard that some of what was left of the liquor spilled out onto his desk, narrowly missing her bag. "You're not too early because either you're playing games or you're a lying, unfaithful bitch! And you had the nerve to want Casey in on this?"

Ivan was stunned at the turn of events, but decided his intrusion might cause more harm than good. He'd stand by in case the altercation built to a dangerous level, but he knew that Otto's bark was way worse than his bite.

"What are you talking about? I've never seen you like this. You're scaring me and how on earth can you speak to me like that or even think that I'd be unfaithful to you," she said, beginning to cry. Her face was devoid of all color and her hands trembled as she reached for the lace handkerchief in her purse.

Otto swatted aside the bag and almost dragged his wife to the small sofa where he pushed her down into it. She sat motionless while he stomped back and forth gearing up for the next installment of his accusations. Desiree huddled back into the cushions like an obedient puppy, her eyes glazed over, and not daring to say a further word. She almost wished Ivan hadn't left the room, but by now he must have reached his office at the end of the hall where Emily was patiently waiting for him.

"I'm not saying everything was your fault. I'll give you the benefit of the doubt, but I need to know what's going on between you and Casey. Ivan followed you downtown and spotted you at the Ritz-Carlton, of all places. Why were you there? Were you meeting someone for lunch? Or, is it Casey you were meeting?" Otto said, grilling her. "Couldn't you at least have picked a less conspicuous spot?"

Somehow Desiree found her voice and took the offensive with her husband, who seemed to be grinding his feet into the old area rug.

"Exactly what are you getting at? You think I'm involved with Casey? To a degree I am, but not in the way you mean. Honey, I love you. He's the last person I'd be interested in, even if I were single. You've got to be kidding."

"No, my dear, I am dead serious. Ivan saw both of you. He followed you to the Ritz. Okay, I understand how you could be flattered by Casey's attention, but that still doesn't give you the right to meet him in a hotel. What if our friends saw you together? How does that look? I want some answers, now."

In the course of ten minutes, Desiree's demeanor had gone from shock to fear, and then to calm. Now, she was downright confused.

"Ivan did what? Why? What's going on here?"

Ivan, who'd witnessed the entire scene, began to perspire. He hadn't wanted his involvement revealed to Desiree. Surely he must have mentioned that to his brother. He and Emily had struggled to reach a point where the two couples were progressing in their relationship, and Otto was inadvertently undermining that. They'd be back to square one, and the chances of rebuilding a connection would be trashed.

He knew that Desiree had recently taken home an expensive Wolf Kahn pastel on approval, and she'd made certain that Emily was at the gallery that day to receive the commission and not Brent. Now that Otto pointed out how instrumental Ivan had been in what led to this diatribe, they could kiss that big commission goodbye. Desiree would certainly return the piece, and probably never set foot in the gallery again. He heard his brother continue on, and the handwriting was on all four walls. He'd never be able to make it up with Desiree. His only hope was that Otto would remove Casey if he even held on to the slightest doubt about their dalliance. Ivan would still be able to advance in the company with Casey gone.

"I asked him to keep an eye on the two of you after he told me about his suspicions, so he followed you," Otto said, crossing his arms and looking down on his wife. "And it's a good thing I okayed it because for once my little brother was right. But like I said, I'll give you the benefit of the doubt and let Casey take the blame for this. He'll be fired as of tomorrow. Oh, don't worry. He'll get a generous severance package and even a letter of recommendation. I just don't want to see his face around here ever again."

"Otto, you're not making sense. Why exactly was Ivan following me? And what are you blaming Casey for? I'm really in the dark as to what you're talking about. Please, clue me in," Desiree said trying to coax her husband back down to earth.

"I'm blaming him for getting you into bed, or trying to. Let me tell you one thing. Not only is he going to be out of Blackmoor Industries, but he's also out of your life as of this minute. I need your promise that you'll never see him again because our marriage is more important than a fling with a man who's acting inappropriately toward you."

Chapter Nineteen

AS THE STOMACH TURNS

"Trifles light as air are to the jealous confirmations strong as proofs of holy writ..."

Ivan breathed a sigh of relief that the discussion had reverted to Casey, and not to him. Maybe there was still a shred of a chance that he and Emily could reestablish their connection with Desiree. He'd have a lot of apologizing to do, and hopefully, Desiree would relent. It was going to be alright if only Otto would fire Casey and get Desiree to stop seeing him. Why did she need him as a friend in the first place? Casey was close to Emily and had been for years. Did Desiree have to horn in on that too?

Bitch!

Ivan knew there was probably nothing going on between them, and clearly she loved Otto. When he thought the conversation in Otto's office had finally quieted down he decided to leave his secretive post and head back to his own office where Emily was waiting.

Then he heard Desiree explode.

"What are you talking about? You are so out of line, and I don't know what Ivan could have possibly told you that you'd have him spy on me. He was right about something, because I did meet Casey at the Ritz, and if you'd give me two minutes to explain, you'll see how innocent it all was. I'll deal with that brother of yours another time, but for sure, that painting I bought is going back in the morning. I went out of my way to get to the gallery when Emily was there and he can damn well try to explain to his wannabe social climbing wife why she lost out on a big commission."

Ivan's stomach did a flip hearing Desiree's last remark. She'd never forgive him now, and her goodwill toward Emily would cease. Desiree could probably teach Donald Trump a thing or two about building a wall to keep people out.

Ivan knew he'd screwed up that part of the deal, but Casey's demise from the company was still in the works.

"What can you explain? That you've finally gotten tired of me? That Casey took advantage of a young, beautiful, vulnerable woman?" Otto said, looking forlorn. He sank down into the sofa and put his head in his hands.

"Sweetheart, you really have to calm yourself and listen to me," Desiree said, putting her hand on his trying to assuage her husband's pain. "It's not at all what you think."

There must have been something in her tone that Otto perceived as condescending because he flung her hand away and jolted up from the sofa.

"Should I listen to you prattle on about how you were going to divorce me and take my money so you could carry on with Casey? You'd sure as hell need it because he won't have a penny more from this company. I'll find a way to get out of any severance package and just let him try to get a letter of recommendation from me! If he's this dishonest in his personal life who knows what else he lies about? And you, why you'll get nothing from me either because that's exactly what you deserve! How could you do this to me!"

"Okay, Otto. I've about had it. This conversation is insane and ridiculous, and in a minute, over. There's nothing going on between Casey and me. We are friends, and you know that. Your brother is stirring up trouble for whatever self-serving reason he has, but you simply cannot take his word over mine."

It was too late for Otto to listen to reason. He began his frantic pacing again, kicking aside the damaged rug.

"Why did you tell me you wanted a family? What was that about? Maybe you're already pregnant, with Casey's child. Was that the big rush for us to try? So you could pawn off the bastard as mine?" he said.

Ivan was at the point of interrupting them because his brother sounded like he was about to have a stroke, and he had to try whatever manipulative tactics he could scare up to alleviate the situation. He'd give it another minute. He had to wait until it was firmly established that Casey would be out of the company. Otto had already said as much, hadn't he?

"Are you nuts?" Desiree said, rising from the sofa and standing face to face with Otto. "Wait a damn minute. I think I can guess what this is about. Your lazy brother wants Casey's job and will do or say anything to get it, including having you fire him."

The liquor must have gone to his head, because Otto morphed into a fantasy about his brother's business abilities.

Ivan, barely able to take a breath, loosened his collar. The last thing Desiree needed to hear was about how well he'd been doing as General Manager. That might have worked a day ago, but now it was driving a stake through his heart.

"Ivan should have been made Vice President and I stupidly passed him over. I threw Casey into the spot without even considering my brother, and as of today, he's quite capable of taking over once Casey's gone. Ivan told me that he's carrying a double load, including most of Casey's work. He's plenty able to be second in command. Casey can find a job elsewhere. I won't hold him back...I didn't mean what I said before. He's entitled to his severance and a letter of recommendation, but he is definitely not welcome here anymore," Otto said, in an even tone. He was in control of his emotions now that he had the upper hand.

Ivan's spirits were lifted once again hearing his brother stick up for him, and re-mentioning that Casey would be out. As soon as Casey was gone, Ivan would convince Otto that there'd never been an affair, but that the company would be much better off with the brothers in charge, completing their father's dream. Yes, it would all work out for the best. He'd stay for a few minutes more in case he had to reel in his brother should he go off on another rant, and then pick up Emily and go to dinner. The two of them. There'd be no double dating tonight, or probably ever. He could live with that. A decent trade-off for the important promotion he was about to receive.

"Listen to me," Desiree started in. "This is crazy talk. Get Ivan in here right now because if he has accusations, let him say them to my face, but if you don't mind, I'd like to explain what happened."

"That I'd like to hear and it better be the truth."

"Of course it's the truth, but first, I'd like to remind you of our wedding vows or have you forgotten them?

We were always going to be honest with each other. You told me why Claire asked for a divorce and you swore you'd never behave that way again."

"I remember our vows," Otto said, somewhat abashed.

"I never wanted to end up with a jealous monster, which is exactly what you are now."

"Ivan told me things, and wait a minute, how do you explain this?" he said, pulling the mended half-note out of his pocket.

Desiree took hold of the note Otto extended, and briefly scanning it, began to laugh.

"Is this what you're so crazy about? Oh darling, listen to me now. It was all going to be a surprise," she said, walking over to her tote bag to pull out the papers. "Here, for starters, take a gander at these sketches. They're amazing!"

"Why, these look like design sketches for the office renovation."

"Of course that's what they are. Remember Casey said he knew a designer who'd give us fair quotes? These are the preliminaries he did for us and he's giving us a huge discount."

"Okay, I see that, but I still don't understand what you two were doing in the hotel," he said, not willing to let the subject drop.

"Give me a minute, but I need you to promise to keep what I'm going to tell you confidential for the time being."

Once again, Desiree's words hit a sore spot in her husband's emotional psyche and he blew up.

"Confidential? You're giving me orders? I don't think you're in a position to ask any favors of me until we straighten out this whole mess, including what you two were doing at the Ritz. You could have discussed the plans in the boardroom. I'm not paying Casey to take my wife to lunch at the most expensive place in town. Why the hell was that necessary? He told me he was supposed to be meeting a client there. Lies, all lies!"

Ivan, still eavesdropping from his covert station, groaned as he saw his plot disintegrating. He'd have to do some fancy footwork to stay on Otto's good side.

"I'm not lying. We met there because Casey wanted to show me some of the work that the designer did for the hotel lobby, and a few of the executive offices. We grabbed a sandwich at the bar afterwards. It wasn't a big deal. You're blowing it out of proportion."

"It's a big deal to me when I see pictures of my wife kissing a guy in a hotel, especially someone who works directly for me."

"Kissing? Whatever gave you that idea? Oh, I see. Ivan. Where the hell is he? He and that leech wife of his were supposed to meet us back here. God only knows what they're doing in his office. Probably one of her special blow jobs. Oh don't look so surprised. I've caught them at it more than once—behind closed doors."

Desiree headed for the hallway to call Ivan into the office, narrowly missing his presence.

"Ivan! Please come back here now. Oh, there's no way he's going to hear me. Can't you get him on the intercom? But seriously, sweetheart, Casey? You know I don't like men who dress better than I do, although I'd give my eye teeth for that Mark Cross bag of his," she said, giving him what she hoped was a winning smile.

Chapter Twenty

OTTO GOES BALLISTIC

"Dangerous conceits are, in their natures, poisons."

Whether it was the joking around or her laughter that enraged Otto was anyone's guess, but Ivan could see his brother heating up for round three.

"Behind closed doors? The issue is what you and that overpaid executive have been doing behind those doors in hotel rooms. How dare you laugh at me!" he said, nostrils flaring. "I saw the pictures. Do you think my own brother, my flesh and blood, would lie to me? What could he possibly gain from that? He and Emily were the ones who encouraged me to marry you; they're not the ones pulling us apart. It's that fucking Casey. I don't even care if nothing is going on, but you two are way too close and everyone sees it, not just Ivan."

After letting out a deep breath, he was able to feel more relaxed because he had finally put the entire conundrum in perspective.

"I simply cannot tolerate gossip about my wife and an employee, even an important one like Casey Michaels. Anyone could understand that. But I told you I'll forgive you now that we've settled it. You are never to see him again," Otto said, summing up his thoughts.

Desiree began to back away from Otto because although he'd spoken in an eerily calm manner, there was a wild look in his eyes. Both were mannerisms unknown to her in the years they'd been together. He was more frightening to her now than when he'd lost his temper. She would have to settle the situation in her own way when he'd calmed down, and then they'd go on with their lives, yes, even with a little counseling. That certainly couldn't hurt. She wouldn't tolerate any more outbursts like the one today, and decided to take control of the conversation.

"Darling, there really isn't anything to forgive because it's all innocent. Casey and I are friends. Period. You simply can't believe that I have any interest in him. I understand your feelings about the way we act sometimes, and I'll cut that out immediately. I hate to think that I might have embarrassed you.

I love you, and that's the other reason I stopped in to see you," she said. "I have something to tell you."

Ivan pricked up his ears to hear what Desiree was about to reveal, but at that same moment he noticed Bianca walking down the hallway headed his way. He had to waylay her before she reached Otto's office and so he stepped out from his hiding place to casually confront her.

"Bianca, what are you still doing here? It's past five—no need to stay late. We're all done for the day…just waiting for my brother and his wife. We're all going out tonight. I'm sure you have plans," he said, leading her away from his spot.

"I was back in your office talking with Emily. We're going to go shopping together one of these days…I love her fashion sense," Bianca said, hoisting up her padded bra and straightening her skin-tight skirt. "I was going to stop in and say good night to the boss."

"Uh, I wouldn't suggest that…he just told me he needed a few minutes alone with Desiree. That's why I'm hanging out here; waiting for him. It could be a while, you know Otto—a few minutes could turn into twenty. Why don't you take off? Enjoy your evening," Ivan said, hoping he didn't sound too solicitous.

"I guess you're right. I'll let you tell him for me because I have a happy hour date and I don't want to keep him waiting," she said. "Good night!"

"Good night, Bianca. Have a wonderful time and don't make him fall in love with you too quickly!" he said, knowing full well he could always get a laugh out of her.

As soon as she was gone, Ivan returned to his post annoyed that he'd missed part of the conversation, but he'd gotten the bulk of it. As soon as their voices returned to normalcy, he'd step in and let them know it was time to leave for dinner. They couldn't go on fighting much longer.

Maybe I better check with Emily, tell her we'll be ready shortly. I'll grab a coffee while I'm down that way.

"We're going to have a baby!" Desiree told her husband while Ivan was gone. "I took the test this morning and it was positive. It's what we've been hoping for and it's finally happened. We can even stay in the townhome for a year or so. We'll make it work, and I don't want to pressure you into buying a house, but we don't have to talk about that now."

"I'm going to ask for a paternity test," he stated, grabbing hold of her arm and twisting it hard.

"Let go of me! You're insane! You're going to believe what you want to, but I won't stand for it. I'm trying to reason with you, but there's no dealing with you when you're like this. Now I totally understand why Claire left you, and she and I will have a lot to catch up on because I'm going to divorce you also. Oh, by the way, I'm going to have this baby, your baby, on my own. I had a successful career before I met you and I can do it again. Then you and Ivan can have everything you ever wanted. This company! Happy now?"

"You will not divorce me. That will be my decision after the DNA test. Then if the baby proves to be mine, we'll get through this and go on. But I'll tell you one damn thing; if that baby is Casey's, you and 'it' won't get a dime!"

"I'll send you the results after the divorce," she said, trying to extricate herself from his powerful grip. "I won't spend another minute with you. Let me go! You're hurting me. You and your brother can go to hell!" she said, struggling to free herself.

Desiree's remark about banishing the brothers to hell was the first thing Ivan heard when he returned to his spot. He felt dizzy with all the yelling going on and took a step closer so he could partially see and not only hear the action more clearly. He knew it was crucial for him to step in and stop the madness, but first he'd wait for Otto to loosen the stronghold he had on Desiree—then he'd rush in to save the day. She could at least be grateful to him for that. From most of what he could see, Ivan knew that the conversation had escalated out of control. It was a golden opportunity to be the hero in Desiree's eyes by taking her side. He moved his stance to plainly see what would transpire next so he'd be prepared to make the perfect entrance.

"I forbid you to take one step out of this office. You'll leave when I tell you to!" Otto said, and violently shook his wife.

Ivan became physically unable to move as he witnessed the next turn of events in what appeared to be slow motion. His feet felt as if they were trying to move through wet cement. He saw the two tussle, and then Otto slapped his wife so hard that she lost her balance and tripped on the torn rug. As she fell, the side of her head hit the steel work table and she collapsed onto the floor. He saw Otto standing there stunned as he watched the flow of blood spill out onto the same rug.

Ivan's adrenaline raced through his body as he came to full consciousness and practically leaped into the room and over to the body. He felt for a pulse that wasn't there before turning to his brother who seemed to be in a trance.

"Holy Shit, Otto! What have you done? *She's dead!*"

Chapter Twenty-One

DESIREE NO MORE

"So much was his pleasure should be proclaimed."

Although the current state of affairs hadn't played out exactly according to Ivan's scheme, he pole-vaulted to the top of his game and immediately turned the events around to his advantage. Nothing more could be done for Desiree. She was dead. Now it was time to shift gears to secure the coveted business position for himself. If nothing else, Ivan could turn on a dime when it was to his benefit.

"What the hell happened? I heard you yelling and when I got here I saw you fighting with her. I can't believe you actually killed her," he said, obviously not wanting to reveal that he'd witnessed exactly what had happened.

"No! It was an accident. I swear," Otto said, coming out of his daze. "She tripped. Ivan, we've got to do something."

"There's nothing anyone can do, except a coroner. We have to call 911. Otto, can you hear me? It's too late. I'm sorry, but she's dead. What went on? You have to talk to me before anyone else gets here, and we only have a few minutes because Emily is going to come looking for me."

"I told Desiree about the note and accused her of cheating on me. When she denied it I went into a rage. I honestly don't remember what happened next. I do know that she was holding these folders right before we fought. She started to walk out on me, saying she wanted a divorce. I tried to stop her; maybe I pulled her back too hard, but I couldn't let her leave me like Claire did. She must have tripped on the rug. I swear I didn't do anything on purpose. I loved her," Otto said, noticing what was left of his drink that sat on the desk. When he lifted it up, Ivan grabbed it from him.

"Otto, I need you to listen to me very carefully. The police could say you pushed her down and caused her death. You certainly can't have liquor on your breath," he said, and poured the remains down the drain of the wet bar sink.

"Oh my god, the note! Where is it? We can't let anyone see it. That evidence could prove intent. Older man with a young beautiful wife who's having an affair? And even if that part isn't true, a sharp attorney would make mincemeat out of your testimony."

Otto pulled out the crumpled note and handed it to Ivan, who stuffed it into his pocket.

"I loved her; I could never have killed her. It must have been an accident," Otto said, his stilted words coming out in a staccato-like speech pattern.

"Otto, you were fighting with her," Ivan said rather nonchalantly as if it were a given, "and it looked to me like you threw her down."

"No! It wasn't that way at all. What am I going to do? I didn't want to harm her. I never gave her a chance to explain. Ivan, you have to help me fix this," Otto said, his eyes filled with fear.

"Okay, okay, calm down. Let me think for a minute," he said, although he'd already mapped out the whole scheme in his mind. "Here's what's going to happen. We'll say it was an accident when the cops get here; that she tripped and fell before you could grab her," Ivan said.

"I swear, that's exactly the way it happened. One minute she was talking about the office renovations and then she was walking out on me. I only tried to stop her."

"Sure, I believe you, but we'll need more than that. The rug! That's it. Anyone can see what a danger it is. It's obvious from where the body is that she tripped on it. And just this morning I left a call for maintenance to get it the hell out of here. So much damn red tape with those guys—I should have thrown it out myself, but one of the men wanted it for his dog or some such crap. I could have prevented this," Ivan said, with a grunt of disgust.

"No, it's not your fault. It was an accident. If anyone's to blame, it's me," Otto said, coming to his senses and walking over to Desiree's body.

"Stop! Listen to me," Ivan said. "You have to leave everything the way it is. I've seen enough CSI to know that you can't touch anything until the cops get here, even if it's not a crime scene. Here's what we're going to do. I'll say I was in here with you when it happened. It'll be much better that way. Emily won't know that I wasn't because she's still back in my office. You'll need a witness; someone to confirm that it was an accident and that you didn't cause it. That person is me."

"You would do that for me?" Otto said, bemused.

"Of course. We're blood. That's what brothers do for each other. Otto, I'm going to fix this, exactly like you said. Leave it to me because with my help it'll stay a simple accident. It's bad enough that it was fatal, but I can't let you suffer for something you didn't do."

"I don't know how I can ever repay you."

"Let's not worry about that now. I've got to call the police."

As Ivan walked over to the desk phone, Emily appeared in the doorway holding a package.

"Hey, guys. What's taking so long? I'm getting hungry. Where's Desiree?"

"Honey, I was just about to come get you. There's been a terrible accident. Desiree is dead. I've got to call the police," he said, dialing 911.

"What? I just saw her. We came up in the elevator together. I can't believe it. Where is she?" she said, entering the office and spotting the body a second later. "Oh no, what happened? There's blood…"

Ivan silently shushed her so he could give the information to the police, and put up a hand motioning her to stay where she was.

"Sit here," Ivan said, hanging up the phone and pointing to a chair in the corner. "You don't want to be part of the crime scene."

"Crime scene?" Otto said, fading back into a state of shock. "What are you talking about? It was an accident. We had a terrible fight, but I didn't mean for anything to happen. I tried to stop her before she tripped and fell. She hit her head and the blow must have killed her. So much blood…" Otto said, piecing together the story and trying to hold back tears. "Desiree said that nothing was going on…she was trying to explain everything but I never gave her a chance because I kept accusing her. I don't know what happened…"

"He's in shock," Ivan said, breaking in sharply. "He doesn't know what he's saying. I was right here and there was no fight. She tripped on that damned rug and fell hard against the metal table. It happened so quickly we didn't have a chance to grab her."

"Otto, I think you should come away now and wait in the break room until the police arrive. Uh, if there was no argument then there's no need to mention it to anyone," Emily said, sizing up the situation and instinctively knowing that she had to protect Otto. She left the package she'd brought in with her and took Otto by the arm to lead him out.

"No, I can't leave Desiree. I love her. How could I have done this?" he said, unwilling to take a step out of the office.

"You didn't do anything," Ivan said, cutting in. "Otto, you mustn't blame yourself. You got a little excited when Desiree told you how much the office renovation was going to cost, but there was never any kind of an argument. Emily is right. Don't say a word about that. We all loved Desiree. We'd never let anything happen to her if we could help it."

"She was my life."

"The last thing you want is unnecessary questioning. And most important, you have an eyewitness, your brother," Emily said.

Otto tried to speak, but stood there mute.

"He's in shock. We've got to get him to the E.R. as soon as the cops get here, and they are on their way."

Emily, who was as street smart as her husband, added, "You better put a call in to Rodrigo. We need the family attorney here on standby in case they start to question him. He'll know how to handle it."

"I'm on it," Ivan said, pressing their attorney's number into his cell phone.

"I'm so sorry, but don't blame yourself. It was an accident like Ivan said," Emily said, putting her arm around Otto.

"Thank you, Emily. I don't know what I'd do without you and my brother."

"We'll always be here for you. The three of us will get through this together," Emily said, trying to put the vision of dollar signs out of her mind. Otto had always been good to her except for the times when he treated her like an errand girl, evidenced by the bottle of scotch she'd purchased for him today. It would all be worth it once he split the estate. Desiree, sincerely meaning it or not, had recently become more considerate of their relationship and perhaps it would have continued to grow, but it certainly didn't matter now. There was no love lost between the two, but Emily knew that she'd have to beef up her role as the sympathetic sister-in-law in order to keep Otto vested in them as a couple.

After Ivan spoke with the attorney, he and Emily half-carried Otto to the break room so that he could lie down on the long sofa. They had to get him out of his private office before he totally collapsed.

Chapter Twenty-Two

A SIMPLE PLAN

"I am not what I am."

"Once we get him settled, and the police arrive, we'll make sure they take him to the hospital. We'll stay as long as necessary and then I'm taking you out for a much needed drink," Ivan said to his wife, who nodded in agreement.

The paramedics arrived shortly after the police officers. They had been told that it was too late for the victim, but that her husband was in a very bad way. Ivan told them that he didn't want to disturb the process by taking his brother to the E.R., and thought he'd be okay until help arrived. He gave a detailed statement to the police, who seemed satisfied. They would confirm everything with Otto when he was well enough to withstand questioning. Rodrigo arrived and spoke with the police assuring them that Otto would be more than willing to fill in any missing information as soon as he was taken to be medically examined.

The paramedics took over, and after checking Otto's vital signs, they hoisted him up onto a gurney and attached an oxygen mask to his face and brought him downstairs to the ambulance. His blood pressure was dangerously high, and along with a rapid heartbeat, the two medics administered the necessary drugs through an I.V. they'd set up. The sirens blared as they raced to the nearest hospital. Ivan and Emily followed along in their cars.

The doctor on staff continued the I.V., and made sure Otto was stable before admitting him for observation and further testing. The questioning would have to wait.

An hour later, after Ivan saw that his brother was resting comfortably, and practically comatose, he and Emily left to meet up at the 10 Arts Lounge in the Ritz-Carlton. Neither of them had eaten since lunchtime, approximately eight hours ago, and needed sustenance. It had been a grueling afternoon and evening.

"Two dry vodka martinis," Ivan said to the bartender, after he and Emily had left their cars at the valet and seated themselves at the bar. "Would you mind putting in an order for sliders, then we'll look at the menu for a few other appetizers."

"It's been a long day. Thank God Otto is alright, but I'm glad they're keeping him overnight. We both needed this," Emily said, sipping the cocktail that the bartender had mixed with warp speed.

"He's heavily sedated, but I think my statement was enough for the report right now. Rodrigo's handling the paperwork. Otto has a big reputation in this city. I doubt anything more will come of it except a coroner's inquest and there's no way they'll find Otto at fault."

"I don't think your brother could take having to relive the accident; I mean, he may have to sooner or later, but for now, I'm glad you were there. I'm sorry about Desiree, and I know we weren't the best of friends, but this is tragic. She was so young."

"Emily, it wasn't quite a simple accident," Ivan said, happy to have a drink in front of him along with someone he could confide in. It was too big a load to carry by himself.

"What are you talking about? I don't understand. You were standing right next to Otto when I came in."

"You can't tell anyone this but I only said I was in the room to protect my brother. I can tell you one thing; there was a hell of a fight going on, not that I could have prevented her from falling. I was too late for that."

"Holy shit. This is one hot mess now. I told Otto not to mention the argument because you said there wasn't one. I'm so confused. What do you think we should do?"

"Nothing for the moment," Ivan said, deciding to give his wife a partial account of the incident. If she knew he was close enough to have stopped the fight that led up to Desiree's death and hung back instead, who knows what she would think.

"You see, I was nearby when I heard Otto yelling. He loses his temper so often I didn't give it a second thought. It was only when I heard Desiree's practically screaming that I headed back to his office. It all happened so quickly that I didn't have even a second to interfere. He was grabbing her and she was trying to get away from him. Then he gave her a pretty hard smack and that's when she lost her balance and tripped.

It wasn't a true accident because if he'd have left his hands off her, she probably would have been okay. No, he didn't murder her, but the police might not see it that way if they knew the facts. It doesn't matter anyway because we're going to stick to the accident story, and I'm going to stand up for my brother. Otherwise, some prosecutor trying to make his bones could come up with a manslaughter charge, and the last thing we need is a long drawn out trial—even if they find him innocent in the end."

"I can't believe you lied to the police and to Rodrigo. You could be arrested for that and I'm flabbergasted that your brother's going along with you. That goes against who he is."

Ivan shifted in his seat and ordered two more drinks, and something else to eat.

"I didn't exactly lie. I just embellished the story to clear Otto. I left out the part about the argument, so they wouldn't suspect any foul play, and said I was with them the entire time. If I told the cops what I thought happened from what I heard while I was in the hallway, it wouldn't carry the same weight. Do you think I want my brother arrested and thrown in jail? He understands that and we need him in the business. You could say that he caused her death, even if it was unintentional, so I lied for him. If the cops knew he and Desiree were fighting in the office by themselves, who knows what they'd put together."

"I guess I can live with that, but what the hell were they were fighting about? You said something about the cost of the new office furniture, but that doesn't make sense."

"No, it wasn't that. He was jealous of Casey. He believed they were having an affair."

"Don't tell me you mentioned that to Otto," Emily said, exasperated with her husband. "You know what a hothead your brother is. I told you nothing was going on. What I don't know is what you could get out of planting that deception in your brother's mind in the first place. Otto could have a total breakdown," Emily said, not grasping the chain of events that was sure to follow. "We need to keep him on our side…or else you can kiss that money from the estate goodbye. Why did you have to take it further with Casey?"

"Because I've been the lackey long enough in the company. The probate could take months, but if Otto believes in me, he'll up my raise to what it should be and advance us part of the estate money. Without that, we're in limbo. Casey was just a conduit, a means to the end, or in this case, a beginning."

They sat in silence for a few minutes and picked at the food once it arrived. Ivan decided to reveal a few more details to his wife. He would need her compliance going forward so that Otto would accept them as his most trusted allies.

"My brother is sedated right now, but he's tough. I'm sure once he's back at work and comes to his senses he'll make sure that we're equal partners. Who else would lie for him? The hell with Casey. I'm doing half his work anyway, and for your information, I only told my brother the truth about his wife and Casey."

"Oh, Ivan. This could mean a lot of trouble for us. If Otto finds out that nothing was going on, and he will, you'll be out in the street. I think you've made a severe error in judgment. Maybe it's not too late. Let's go back to the station and tell them what really happened. It was still an accident, even with the argument. You did see most of what occurred and you can say you were confused and upset trying to take care of Otto."

"That won't help any of us. Frankly, I don't know if they were having an affair or not, but I saw them in the lobby right here in this hotel, and they looked pretty chummy. Hold on a minute, I forgot about this," he said, and showed her the note which was tucked away in his pocket. "Take a look. What would you have thought? You can read the evidence for yourself, and if the cops ever saw that, Otto'd be sitting on death row even with me as an eye witness. I'm gonna hold on to it for safe keeping in case Casey tries to talk himself back into the company."

"Oh, my god. You've got this all wrong. Believe it or not, Desiree called to tell me she was meeting Casey here so he could introduce her to his friend who's an industrial designer. It was going to be a surprise for Otto. I don't know why she decided to tell me about it, maybe it was an attempt to become better connected as sisters-in law. That's what she must have been discussing with Casey. I told you to back off that affair drama. Desiree is gone and all for nothing, because if Otto finds out that you were in any way involved, we're as dead as she is."

"Listen, I'm sorry about Desiree, but it was my duty to tell my brother what I found. How was I to know what the note meant? But it's not for nothing because something good will come out of it. Casey will be gone and I'll be in. Do you realize what that means? We'll be able to buy whatever house we want and you won't have to count pennies anymore. I'm doing this for us and to save my brother. I've got to keep the note in case Otto decides to change his mind."

"That's called blackmail. Jesus, who writes notes anymore? If only she'd learned how to text none of us would be in this pickle."

"Blackmail is overdoing it, so let's not use that word. Emily, you better back me up on this or Otto will never forgive me. Let him believe that his wife was screwing Casey because that's the only way he'll get rid of him."

"But it's not the truth. Agreed, Desiree wasn't the warmest person in the world, but Otto deserves to know that she was faithful to him. We can't let him go through life thinking otherwise. It'll destroy him, and if it affects business, then all this will be in vain."

"Oh my god, I didn't think that far ahead, but you're right. I'll tell him I found out it was nothing, but not until Casey's gone. Forget going to the police because we'd both be accessories, and then who would profit? Do you really want me out of a job and not getting half of Pop's estate? Do you want Otto suspected of murder? It's your choice, babe. Do you seriously want to live in a shitty condo the rest of your life, or a house in Bryn Mawr?"

Emily plucked the olive out of her Martini and bit into it. The temptation was too great.

"Bryn Mawr? In the estate section? You better give me the note for safe keeping."

"I need you by my side," he said handing her the note. "Nothing will bring Desiree back, and I'm sorry about that, but helping my brother out of a jam will be good for all of us. Honey, I can't get through this alone. I won't let my brother go to jail, or even be part of a trial. The inquest will be tough enough."

"Do what you have to. I'll back you up."

"The main thing is that we all go on, as a family."

Emily started to answer, but instead silently nodded her head in agreement as she pocketed the note.

Chapter Twenty-Three

MEN AT WORK

"My wife, my wife! What wife? I have no wife."

A week later, Otto sat quietly at his desk, mindlessly shuffling through papers when Ivan tapped at the door before joining his brother.

"Come on in. I was hoping you'd stop by. It's been a long day yet somehow the clock only says three."

"Tough one, huh. Otto, it's only been a week. Maybe you shouldn't have come back so soon. No one expected it. First Pop, then Desiree," Ivan said. He empathized with his big brother's pain not only in the loss of their father, but also of his wife. Ivan would be floundering without Emily.

"I thought about taking more time off, but business is my escape, except my concentration is way off. I can't attend to anything of importance, but staying home alone is worse. It's too raw."

"Don't you worry. I'll take care of whatever I can, and I'm sure Casey will do his best as long as he's still here," Ivan said, trying to include his former rival's name into the conversation without stirring up trouble. Ivan had come up with a new proposal that would exonerate Casey from any wrongdoing, and convince Otto to keep him on for the moment.

"This probably isn't the right time, but it doesn't make sense to wait. It's important for you personally and for Blackmoor Industries," Ivan continued, not wanting to lose momentum. "I never should have mentioned the whole thing about Casey and Desiree. First of all, now I'm sure it was all a misunderstanding, and if you fire him for no reason, it could come back to haunt you and we sure as hell don't need a lawsuit from a disgruntled employee. I do feel somewhat responsible, but you have to understand how it looked to me. Why I came to you with the note…"

"Of course, I understand," Otto said, cutting him off. "I miss Desiree more than I can tell you, but I certainly don't hold you accountable because you were only doing your duty, trying to protect me, like any good brother would. That note would have gone a long way in convicting me. Even a kid fresh out of law school could have made a strong case against me."

"Exactly. I hope you know I'd do anything for you, so no worries about the note anymore. That's forgotten because it definitely could have incriminated you, especially if the cops ever found out that you and Desiree had been fighting. If they hadn't believed that I was in your office at the time, it'd be all over. My first instinct was to lie to keep you safe. I know you feel you have to repay me, but we have time to discuss our business relationship. Take a couple of weeks to recover."

"I'm sure you feel bad about lying, but it truly was an accident," Otto said, yawning and stretching his arms overhead. He hadn't had a decent night's sleep in days, and it had taken its toll. Otto, only a few weeks ago, had presented as a healthy vital man in his early fifties, fit in body and mind. Now, he appeared physically and mentally exhausted, and ten years older.

"Of course it was an accident, but why take a chance when it was easier for me to be your eyewitness? There's nothing that can implicate you anymore," Ivan said, knowing that Emily had secreted away the incriminating note.

I doubt I'll have any trouble getting what I want even with keeping Casey on. I'll find some way to finagle the wording. I'll tell Otto that it'd be best for the company if Casey keeps his title—maybe throw him a raise— and make me Executive Vice President until I move up to partner. I'll make sure that Otto believes me about the non-affair business. Shit, there'd be no way I could do what Casey does; I've been blowing smoke up my brother's ass to impress him. Otto's in such a slump now and useless, so we'll need Casey more than ever.

"I do want to repay you for saying you were with me when it happened. The police believed everything, and Rodrigo took care of all the details and the inquest. I don't know how I could have managed this whole ordeal without you and Emily. It would've been so much worse if the police thought I had anything to do with it. Thank God they never saw that note," Otto said, repeating his earlier sentiments, and appearing grateful to his brother for saving his skin.

"I told you, we'll work something out here in the company. Sure, I could have been truthful with the cops, but that wouldn't serve any purpose and you can do far more here than sitting in a jail cell," Ivan said, playing the savior.

"You and Emily have both been wonderful. She even brought lunch over to the house a couple of times on her way to the gallery. We've had some good talks. She's been like a therapist for me."

"Emily's great that way. And Otto, don't forget, you've always taken care of us. I wanted to prove my loyalty to you. That's what family is for."

"I won't forget what you did, and I'll take that into account sooner rather than later. Say, how about a drink?"

"I thought you were out of scotch," Ivan said, anxious to hear what Otto was referring to.

"Emily brought up a bottle the day...the day

Desiree died. She must have opened it while I was still at home after the hospital. Hah! Even transferred it to a decanter. I'll pour."

"Isn't it kind of early in the day for that? It's only a little after three," Ivan said, glancing at the new Cartier Tank watch he'd treated himself to while awaiting his share of their father's will. He and Emily would be able to pay off all their credit card bills once the money was in their account and then buy the home they should be living in. Emily had even suggested that they join the local country club.

"Didn't you tell me it's five o'clock somewhere? Come on, relax a little," Otto said, perking up, and straightening his shoulders. Suddenly, the tension was gone from his expression, and his step was jaunty as he walked to the liquor cabinet.

"Otto, are you feeling okay? You're not acting entirely rational," Ivan said, a perplexed look on his face. A minute ago it seemed as if Otto was in a deep depression, ready to give up on everything; now he seemed like he was on top of the world.

"I'm more myself than you know, and why not? What's done is done, and we have some celebrating to do," Otto said.

Ivan, nervous that someone might walk by, sprung up from his chair and scanned the hallway to make sure no one was around. He closed the door just in case one of the employees decided to pay their boss a visit to console him. He certainly couldn't chance that

Casey would choose this time for a meeting. He'd have to count on his brother's secretary, Bianca, to keep all sympathizers at bay. The brothers had to look bereft after the recent events.

"Otto, celebrating isn't exactly an appropriate word right now. You wouldn't want anyone to hear you talking like that. I'm going to tell Bianca to hold all calls, and not to let anyone come into your office. I'll be right back."

"Yes, you do that. I'll be waiting."

In the few minutes that Ivan was gone, Otto filled two bar glasses with the scotch that Emily had picked up for him, and added ice, but no water. He suspected she hadn't bought his usual brand because she'd taken the liberty of transferring the liquor to the decanter that Otto's father kept in the back of the bar, but never used.

"Okay. Bianca is on it and I stopped at Casey's office to tell him you weren't up to a meeting today. Otto, I'm a little worried about you because this isn't normal behavior. Sad, then happy…maybe you should see a grief counselor…"

"The hell it isn't normal," Otto broke in sharply. "You should have invited that son of a bitch in because I'm going to fire the bastard. Here, take your drink."

"Whoa, hold on there a minute. That's what I started to tell you before. I want to clear up the whole situation and tell you why he was at the Ritz with Desiree, and it's not at all what we first thought. Please listen to me for a minute because now is not the time to chuck him. He does carry a lot of knowledge that I'm still learning and you sure as hell don't want a bad reputation on your hands for indiscriminately letting someone go. Why not leave him as V.P., give him a boost in pay, and maybe make me partner," Ivan said, sneaking in his wish to advance himself even further.

There! It's out on the table and it's what he should do for me considering what I did for him! My reward for keeping him out of jail.

Ivan was nervous thinking about Casey being fired, which would disrupt the company business, and eventually Otto would hold him accountable for getting rid of the one person they needed the most. "Partner? That's an idea," Otto said, without committing himself to the promotion.

"And give Casey a raise?" Otto continued. "My, my, aren't you feeling magnanimous toward the person responsible for Desiree's death."

"What? Casey wasn't even here when it happened. How could he have anything to do with it?" Ivan asked.

"Hold that thought because the decorating story was a cover-up all along. She was cheating on me with him. You have good instincts about people. I only wish I had seen it sooner."

"A cover-up? Seriously?" Ivan said, pumping himself up after recovering. "You mean I was right about them?"

"Of course, you were right. I'm not stupid; there was no misunderstanding with those office plans. You had it down the first time you came to me. She was definitely screwing him."

"This is confusing because Emily mentioned those sketches to me," Ivan said. "That's what I've been trying to tell you. Desiree and Casey were working with some dude about redecorating the office. That's why they met at the Ritz, at least, that's what I thought until you just put it together for me. Funny thing about the note; it was innocent. Desiree just wanted to confirm her appointment with Casey. Looks like she had us all fooled."

"I'm sure she was planning on some changes around here, so she'd have a good cover story for seeing Casey. Ironic, isn't it? The one item they should have junked was the rug that killed her. The official report said it was an accident, like we told them, so let sleeping dogs lie," Otto said, almost as a command.

"I should have known you were too smart not to see what was going on, and I'll bet Casey won't even have the guts to own up to the affair. It was all his fault, and I've been kicking myself for getting involved. Even fought with Emily over it. She swore they weren't doing anything but business. I know I should have come clean about all this a week ago but I was afraid you'd blow up at me. Jesus, what a clusterfuck this is."

"Don't be too angry with your wife or Casey, and

you're right about keeping him on at least until we can replace him. He did me a favor. My precious wife got what she deserved, and I didn't have to spend a dime. We never had a pre-nup, and a divorce would have cost me a fortune. I just got lucky with the accident. Come to think of it, I really owe it all to you. If you hadn't have grabbed that note in the first place after you saw them at the Ritz, I never would have figured it all out. Come on, Ivan, join me in a drink," Otto said with gusto. "Then, we'll go over our future together."

Chapter Twenty-Four

DON'T DRINK
AND WORK

*"In following him I follow but myself; heaven is my judge,
not I for love and duty."*

Ivan sipped his drink, the taste somewhat unfamiliar.
He wondered if Emily had purchased a cheaper
brand and pocketed the extra money Otto had most
likely given her. Ivan only saw a decanter on the
bar counter, and not the actual bottle. He'd have to
question Emily on that because there was nothing to
be gained being penny wise and pound foolish when
it came to relatively small items like a premier bottle
of liquor.

"Our future? Right!" Ivan said, envisioning the new
sign on his office door. "You know, maybe you're right
about all this, but I still don't understand what we're

celebrating. I mean with Desiree dead, it doesn't look right. What if someone had peaked in? They'd see you in pretty high spirits."

"True, but they'd see me sitting here and having a drink with my new partner! That is the position you wanted, isn't it Why stop at Vice President?"

"Oh, hey Otto, that really is something. I may not be as smart as Casey, but I'm a hard worker, and more important, you can trust me one hundred percent. And don't forget, Emily and I are going to be around for you all the time," he smiled and lifted his glass. "To us. And sure, keep Casey on. Why not?"

Otto lifted his glass and joined his brother in a toast. If Ivan didn't know what a straight arrow his brother was, he would have sworn that he'd taken a happy pill. He had to keep the staff away from Otto's office, and with that idea in mind he made his excuses and stepped out into the hallway and told Bianca it was fine to dismiss everyone. It was Friday, after all, and everyone needed a break.

"Otto, as my first official duty I told Bianca we're closing early today. You and I can stay and talk, but I think the rest of our employees wouldn't mind an extra hour or two added to their weekend," he said. "I guess I should've asked you first, but I think it's for the best. You don't mind, do you?"

"Not at all. Good idea. They deserve it. I couldn't ask for a more loyal group."

"Before we discuss anything else, business I mean,

I'd like to clear something up. Tell me, and I don't want to belabor the point, but how exactly did you find out they were screwing around? The note was so ambiguous," Ivan said, sipping more of his cocktail. Now he was sure it wasn't the usual brand, but it was certainly drinkable. He'd have to warn Emily not to try to pass off a cheaper brand again.

"Oh, right, almost forgot that part of the story, but I'll get to it in a minute. Good scotch, by the way, isn't it? Let me give you a refill."

"Funny you should ask because I find it's a bit different this time—a little smokier. What's the label? It doesn't taste quite like the stuff Pop used to have," Ivan said, beginning to feel drowsy. "Wow, it's got a kick to it."

"I assume it's the same good hooch. Emily said she would come back to the office while I was at home and unpack it. I told her Bianca would set it up, but she insisted on doing it herself. She must have poured it into the decanter when she was here and ditched the bottle. Pop never used it, but it's Baccarat crystal, no lead, if that's what you're worried about."

"I remember that decanter. Emily and I gave it to Pop for his birthday one year. He barely said thanks."

"Maybe you're tired from all the stress of the inquest, and your work around here, so it's hitting you harder. But you know what? I think it's wiping me out too. Come on over to the sofa and we'll discuss the note."

Ivan instinctively thought about the note that Emily was keeping, secure in the fact that Otto would never see it, unless it was necessary to sustain his new position in the company. If Otto didn't come through with his promises, he could easily embroil him in a scandal, although he'd have to admit his part in the story, but what judge or jury wouldn't understand that he'd acted out of love for his brother? The scotch was hitting him with full force and he gratefully stumbled over to the sofa.

"We don't have to do this if it's too painful. We both know what the note said, at least the part that I had. Don't torture yourself. It's over now," Ivan said, his eyes heavy.

Otto ignored Ivan's slurred words and reached into one of the file drawers where he pulled out the other half of the note.

"Ivan, look what I have!" Otto practically sang out. "Remember the first part of the note? Something about their meeting at the same place, and all that? Well, here's the rest of it. Let me read it to you because you don't look so good. I'm a little tired myself, but we have to get through this. 'I can't wait to see Otto's face when we show him the sketches for the offices. Thanks so much for introducing me to William. What a terrific guy and he'll be just the right designer for the company. Desiree.'"

"Hey Otto, what's going on? I saw them and you just said they were carrying on. What's the deal? Are you trying to trap me into saying something? And who the fuck is William?" Ivan managed to sputter out.

"It seems, dear brother, that your nemesis is gay. William is Casey's partner."

"Casey? Gay? Holy shit. I had no idea," Ivan started to say, his tongue thick.

"What's the matter, oh dear brother of mine? Can't hold your liquor?" Otto said. "I'm feeling pretty woozy myself, but while I still have strength, I'll finish the story. Emily went to Casey after the inquest and told him about your suspicions and mentioned the note or what she remembered of it. He told her he was wondering what happened to it, and showed her the second half. He never shared his personal life with any of us although no one here would have cared. He only told Desiree because he figured she'd be working with William, and there was no reason to keep it a secret any longer. Emily's known for ages."

"I don't understand why she didn't tell me Casey was gay. I don't care about people being gay, straight, trans or whatever," Ivan said, becoming more and more befuddled.

"Your wife loved you, but she never trusted you. She knew you were gunning for Casey's job and you'd use any ammunition you could against him, including spreading vicious rumors like you did about his relationship with my wife. Like you said, no one here would have cared unless you decided to turn it into something ugly. He's been a remarkable employee even though you're doing half of his work,"

Otto said, with a heavy dose of sarcasm. His voice was becoming weaker as he went on with the story.

Ivan sat almost stupefied, and then gathered up what remaining strength he had to stagger over to the bar. Almost zombie-like, he poured another glass of scotch not bothering to add ice.

"My wife betrayed me," he said simply.

"After Emily spoke to Casey, she knew I'd want to see the note to clear up any remaining doubts I might still have had, and to explain about William. You divided this family, which makes you the real killer. You caused the death of my wife and my unborn child, that's right, Ivan. Desiree was pregnant. She told me that day."

"I swear I didn't know about the baby," Ivan said, the thought passing through his muddled brain that he'd missed that part of the conversation when Bianca had interrupted him. "You can't mean what you said, that I'm the killer. You're not going to go to the police with all this, or to Rodrigo, are you? Emily knows I wasn't in the room when Desiree died—you'd be implicating her too. We've all perjured ourselves so you wouldn't be charged with manslaughter," he said, barely able to put his words together, and not even sure if he'd spoken them. He began to sweat profusely and tried to loosen his tie, but his fingers weren't working. Something was not right. His throat was closing up, and in an attempt to soothe it, he downed the rest of the liquid in the glass.

"Emily did what she thought she had to, for my sake, and most likely mainly for hers, but unfortunately not yours," Otto said with a nasty tinge. "She did betray you and although I was relieved to find out that there was nothing between Casey and Desiree except friendship, your wife's loyalty act stinks to high heaven. Oh, what I told you about splitting the estate? That's not happening. She'll get nothing, and you won't need it where you're going."

"Otto, listen here," he said, swaying back and forth before plunking back down on the small sofa. "Emily's a pretentious bitch and she's always been jealous of Desiree. She almost went to the police to get you in big trouble, but I talked her out of it the night Desiree died. You're right! She doesn't deserve a thing! But we're brothers! Blood," he managed to get out. "I'll divorce her and work my ass off here to prove myself. I'll do whatever it takes, but you have to promise not to go to the police. Like you said, let sleeping dogs lie…we don't want to end up in jail."

"Don't worry, Ivan, you're not going to jail, nor will I. No court of law would ever convict you although they might charge me with manslaughter. You'd go free and I couldn't allow that to happen. Desiree was innocent. My life means nothing without her and I was stupid enough to believe you and your lies. Now I can't live with myself anymore, and you don't deserve to live either."

"But the business! We'll work side by side and everything will get back to normal. You can't let the business die."

"Don't worry, little brother, the business won't die, but you and I shall. You see, like I said, Emily brought the scotch to the office the day Desiree died, and returned to decant it when I wasn't here. When I saw she'd decided to use the Baccarat, most likely to disguise the fact that she skimped on the brand, I added a little something extra for a dramatic exit. In a minute you'll pass out and you'll be dead within the hour judging from the amount you drank. I'll follow shortly, and later this evening the cleaning staff will find both of us dead. In my safe deposit box there is a registered letter and instructions for Rodrigo to set Casey up as owner and president of the company. Casey always was the best man for the job."

"But what about me? I'm going to be your partner," Ivan croaked out, his last words on the subject, and on earth.

Otto never heard him.

EPILOGUE

*"Not poppy, nor mandragora, nor all the drowsy syrups
of the world, shall ever medicine thee to that
sweet sleep which thou owedst yesterday."*

The brothers indeed looked like they were napping, Ivan slumped over on the sofa and Otto slanted back in his chair. The cleaning crew wouldn't arrive for several hours, and no one else was in the office after Bianca had dismissed the staff earlier in the day.

"Hello, anyone home?" Emily called out.

The door was open so she entered taking in the scene.

"Oh, you guys. How much have you been drinking?" she said, assuming they were asleep. "I see you were kind enough to leave an ounce or two for me. Some power nap. You look like you're totally out of it."

I can't wait to tell the guys what a fantastic day I had at the gallery. Two pieces to the same buyer and he's coming back once we restock the pastel that her royal highness returned. Otto won't mind celebrating our good fortune even though he's still mourning Desiree. He needs to eat, and I need to pretend like I still care.

"Hey, you guys. Wake up! I know you weren't expecting me this early but I have some great news. I guess I have to toast by myself and then I'm dragging you both out to dinner," she said, pouring the balance of the scotch into the glass and quickly draining it of its contents.

Whew, no wonder those guys are out cold. I shouldn't have bought the cheaper brand just to pocket the extra twenty bucks. It's a good thing Otto never saw the bottle. This stuff could strip paint.

A deep fatigue engulfed her slim frame and she fell into one of the office chairs not even able to reach the sofa.

I'll just rest my eyes for a minute.

ACKNOWLEDGMENTS

My thanks to the Palm Beach and Broward County Libraries, the National League of American Pen Women, Women's National Book Association, Florida Mystery Writers and the South Florida Theatre League for their support. Unending gratitude goes to Murder on the Beach Mystery Book Store for their hospitality. To Benjamin Laskin, who writes the most incredible books; thank you for the fun email exchange and your encouraging words. To director Genie Croft and producer Keith Garsson for their expert theatrical advice, and to the cast of my play, *Text M for Murder,* from which this book is adapted. Last but never least, to Penelope Love, friend and editor, who makes it all possible.

READERS' GROUP GUIDE

1. Do you feel that Otto, Sr., was fair to leave his entire estate to Otto, Jr., or should he have split it between his two sons?

2. Have you ever had a job with a family member in charge? If so, how did it work out?

3. Do you think Emily meant to betray Ivan by showing Casey the note? How else could she have handled the situation so as not to have alienated her husband?

4. Desiree and Emily are both motivated by love and money. Which do you think is more important to each?

5. Did you think that Casey and Desiree may have been having an affair?

6. Which, if any, of the characters did you have empathy for?

7. Discuss the similarities in this book as they relate to Shakespeare's play *Othello*.

8. Did you anticipate the twist at the end?

Thank you for reading A Divided Duty. If you enjoyed this story, please support the author's efforts by helping other readers find this book. Here are some suggestions for your consideration:

* Write an online customer review.

* Gift a copy of this book to a booklover friend.

* Visit Carol's website or email her at polowhite@aol.com

www.carolwhitefiction.com

* Spread the word about her work. Suggest her titles to a local book club.

* For group orders of ten books or more, contact Citrine Publishing at (561) 299-1150 or Publisher@CitrinePublishing.com.